Jameson
15322 Saint Jameson Rd
Culpeper VA 22701-1380

The Last Valentine

JAMES MICHAEL PRATT

DOUBLEDAY DIRECT LARGE PRINT EDITION

St. Martin's Press ⌇⌇ New York

Grateful acknowledgment is given for permission to reprint lyrics from the song "Traces." Writers: Bule/Cobb/Gordy Publisher: Low-Sal Inc. Copyright © 1969.

ISBN 0-7394-0680-9

**This Large Print Book carries the
Seal of Approval of N.A.V.H.**

For Jeanne,
who has walked with me
through the "Tunnel of Love."

Contents

Acknowledgments

A profound sense of gratitude fills me when I realize *The Last Valentine* began as a devoted son's gesture of respect for his deceased father, and for his mother, who exemplify the beliefs and highest expression of love portrayed by the characters in this book. I will never be able to show them enough thanks for the example they set in their devotion to each other for fifty years, as well as to their family and friends. I could not have evoked the emotions necessary for this creative task without having their constant living example before me.

My father's final three words in life were heard by me alone. I held his hand, saying good-bye to the voiceless man who was struggling to breathe his last breaths. Almost as if from the very brink of death, he aroused himself one final time. His breathing eased, his eyes turned my way. He voiced his first distinct words in over a week. His final "I love you!" was whispered to me as my deaf mother kissed his cheeks and stroked his head.

"You can go now, Grant," she said. "I love you so much! You can go now." Any gift they gave me could never exceed the one I was given that day in witnessing that last moment, the final gift of love.

A special thanks goes to all who supported my work early on. From the time I was honing my skills in building a business, to my dream of "building stories that would lift and inspire others," many encouraged me as a career transition was made. It could not have happened without the belief of my wife, Jeanne, and of my children, Michael and Amy, who cheered me on every step of the way.

My other family members, including brothers Rex, Grant Jr., and Nick—former business partners—offered continual encouragement and support. John and Janean Hendrickson offered unsolicited backing, which made it possible for *The Last Valentine* to be sent out into the world, selling over 10,000 copies in a matter of months through a small independent distributor, Origin Book Sales. I offer my deepest respect and thanks to them, along with Michael Hurst and the staff at Origin for their constant faith and devoted energy in placing that first self-published printing on bookstore shelves.

The writer could not have developed his sense of fiction that inspired without the mentoring and first editing of author and friend Hartt Wixom. Others, including Stevens W. Anderson and Darla Isackson, contributed their skills and belief. To AEI editor and friend Andrea McKeown, who has taken many hours to review and work closely with me, a special "thank you!"

Finally, my sincere appreciation is reserved for Kenneth J. Atchity, author and literary manager, a man who understands a writer's dreams and who skillfully blends his expertise in the craft with the task of representation. Ken Atchity and partner,

Chi-Li Wong, of Atchity Editorial/Entertainment International, Inc., of Los Angeles and New York are truly "dream makers."

I offer my gratitude to St. Martin's Press, especially Jennifer Enderlin, Executive Editor, whose belief, enthusiasm, skills, and vision brought *The Last Valentine* to the reader today. Thank you!

Introduction

Once in a while, our thoughts drift and fade, back into the recessed hiding places where our memories are safely stored. At times we recall them—the memories of our loves, our youth, our life experiences. These dreams appear to us, day or night, and for seconds, minutes, or hours we are there once again.

Memory. Our mind's powerful possessor of personal events. Powerful enough to remind us, teach us, hold us slaves, or free us. Memories of the past are forever suspended in our minds for instant recall and can have the power to possess our present lives.

Memories of love—no matter how distant the scene—can once again bring to us the sweet joys of youth, just as it was *then.* No matter our age, we all sometimes long for things to be as they were *then,* when there were endless possibilities, when life was beginning and anything seemed ours for the taking.

The Last Valentine is a story about memories of love—love, the romantic kind—love, the brotherly kind—love, the kind that endures trial and, in devotion, becomes never ending in its loyalty.

In the end, it's about love that gains immortal stature. Like a torch that cannot be extinguished, this kind of love transcends time to touch the lives that seek it.

Along with our memories of loving relationships, there are often special places, both public and private, that captivate and hold a sacred meaning for us. In recalling these places, our memories evoke reverent feelings—not because the places themselves are holy sanctuaries, but because something wonderful—heavenly—happened there.

So it was with Lt. Neil Thomas, Sr., USN, and his wife, Caroline. So it is with the story of *The Last Valentine.*

A Love Story

Susan Allison guided the rented Lexus slowly down the quiet, magnolia-lined Pasadena street, her fingernails tapping in annoyance against the console as she tried to read the house numbers passing by. Her body, clothed in a black silk suit, was like a perfectly sculpted ornament on the sea of leather, as if the car's designers had deliberately added her as a final finishing touch. Susan felt comfortable here, cocooned within the solid steel frame of the Lexus with its immaculate interior, where the turmoil of the city life outside could not penetrate. The world inside this car was the world Susan had built for herself. She felt safe here—safe, but irritated.

If the assignment had been politics, or a Death Row interview, or a trip to Bosnia or Lagos or Damascus, she would've gladly dropped everything at the last minute. But this! How could they send her to cover some love story? There were plenty of people who liked love stories, who cared about them, who believed in them. Who made more sense for this chore. For Susan, a story like this was a waste of her time. Fluff. But she had to be in Southern California anyway to put the finishing touches on her health care exposé at their Los Angeles affiliate station, CNTV. So she had agreed to satisfy Craig Warren's curiosity by checking out this Neil guy before returning to Baltimore. What real choice did she have? No one could say no to Craig.

At the end of the block she found the house. She pulled into the driveway and stopped. A strange feeling stole over her as her eyes took in the white picket fence, the perfectly manicured lawn, the bursting flower beds in front of the house and along the walk, and the magenta bougainvillea over the front door. For a second, she almost lost sight of where she was, of what she had come to do.

At that moment, the front door opened. A man stepped outside into the cloud-shadowed sunlight. Susan forced herself to get out of the car. As she walked toward the house, the brightly colored California poppies along the walkway seemed to bend to brush her ankles. She smiled and gave her hand to the tall, well-proportioned, neatly dressed man waiting to greet her at the front door of this storybook house. "Hi, I'm Susan Allison," she said.

"It's a pleasure to meet you, Ms. Allison. I'm Neil Thomas."

"I hate to start out on a negative note," she began as he led her inside. She'd hesitated at first, standing on the front step, staring at the yard, the building, the flower beds. They seemed familiar somehow. "But you seem like a nice man, and I want to be honest with you," she went on, taking a seat on the sofa in front of the bay window, ignoring the packing boxes scattered around the room. "This really isn't my kind of story."

He had followed her into the living room, sitting down in the armchair facing her across the coffee table. "I appreciate your honesty," he said. "You can count on the same from me."

"Thank you. So tell me your story. When my managing editor saw the article about it in your local paper, he told me not to come home until I came out here to see you. It must really be something."

"It is. My parents were special people. They were well-loved in this old neighborhood."

"So you've written a story about their wartime romance?"

Neil leaned forward, smiling. "I don't know about the writing. I did the best I could, but I honestly believe it's the most inspirational love story you'll ever hear."

Susan remained serious. "Great," she said. "That's why I'm here."

"I pieced it together from the letters my parents wrote to each other," he began, "and from interviews with the people who were there. Perfect love is a lofty goal, but if anyone ever reached it in their lifetime, my parents did."

Susan almost flinched at the words,

shifting her eyes toward the antique crystal clock sitting next to a packing box on the mantel.

"The story spans five decades," Neil went on. "It's about promises kept and devotion to cherished dreams."

Susan was struggling to keep her attention focused.

"Wait. I've got a better idea," he said, as if he'd sensed her reaction. He opened the box containing his writing, reached in, then extended a few pages across the coffee table toward her. "Here. Why don't you read this much? If you don't want to hear the rest of it after that, we'll shake hands and go our separate ways."

Susan couldn't look him in the eyes now, afraid that she wouldn't be able to restrain herself from saying what she really thought about this story. But she did have a job to do, plus he seemed so sincere. She finally accepted them, laying them on the sofa beside her without saying a word, oblivious to the awkward silence.

"It's only a few pages," Neil said, rising. "Why don't you take a look at them while I make us some coffee?"

As he headed into the kitchen, Susan sighed and picked them up.

February 14, 1994
Amtrak's Union Station, Los Angeles, California

It had been exactly fifty years since she'd seen him. He was home on leave, a U.S. Navy pilot, before shipping out to the fight that was raging in the Pacific. To her, he epitomized the word handsome, especially in his white dress uniform, his jet black hair combed in that carelessly meticulous Clark Gable way. A perfect toothy smile complemented the blue eyes that held her as easily as his muscular arms. But beyond her physical attraction, she was drawn to Neil most by his tenderness, his thoughtfulness, his wit. He made her smile through gloom; he laughed at his own mistakes and bad luck. "Bad luck can't be all bad," he'd say, "since I've never really had any luck at all."

She loved his ready solutions to problems, the way he worked at something until he had it. She felt loved, not only for all the little things he did for her, but because he made her feel wanted and needed.

It wasn't just this place, the old train station, that made the flood of memories return, but the fact that they had touched each other for the last time here, before his train had pulled away. Then, as always during the few short months they'd been together, his touch had been magical, like nothing she'd ever experienced before. When Neil held her, she felt safe. The world seemed right.

The old woman imagined she could see him there, just as he had been then, waving to her as he boarded the train.

Caroline clutched his last letter in her hand as she walked through the glass doors into the massive lobby of the old depot on Alameda Street. The station was cathedral-like, a California Spanish colonial architecture with a Catholic mission flavor, the ones built by Catholic priests in the late seventeen and early eighteen hundreds that dotted the California coast. It felt like home to her.

Union Station had been brand-new then, when she'd entered these doors to send her husband off to war. It seemed even larger now, now that it was so empty. Now that the crowds had diminished. She liked it that way, though, as if her special place was theirs alone, this place that seemed frozen in time.

She shuffled past the photo gallery on the lower walls of the fifty-foot-high lobby, under its massive beams and huge candelabra lights. The subdued glow of overhead lighting mixed with the light from outside. The shafts of light streaming in made the polished mosaic-tile floor glisten enticingly, inviting visitors to linger and gaze at the photographs.

The old photos, encased in glass-covered frames, displayed a history of the years of construction, especially the war years. Union Station was running at peak capacity for travelers, especially soldiers embarking into the unknown.

She stopped as she always did in front of the last photo on the north wall, by the old ticketing area, which was now closed. There it was: mobs of soldiers. Sailors, marines, their girls, heading out to gates G and H, and the tunnel leading to track number twelve. She was there, in the picture, if one looked hard enough. At twenty-three, with twenty-five-year-old Neil. He was turned to one side, looking down at her.

A photographer had captured the moment. She had relived it over and over again. She ached for him now as she reached her aged hand out to gently caress the old glass-covered photo, as if in touching it she could erase the fifty years that separated them.

But today she was happy. He would come today. She knew he would. She had seen the swallow in the window yesterday, and she held his last letter now.

The royal red roses he'd planted all those years before had survived. They'd bloomed early this year, as they had the day he went away, on their first wedding anniversary, the 14th of February 1944. It was a sign that he hadn't forgotten, that he would come for her. Even if it was only a dream, she would be happy to be so deluded.

She stared at the photo, with one last hard look, remembering how heart-breaking it had been to finally say good-bye.

She hadn't made it easy for Neil. He'd tried to leave her gently. She re-membered being an emotional wreck. As she thought back to that day, she imagined hearing his voice again. She closed her eyes to savor the memory, pretending to touch him. Mentally, she was a girl once more, revisiting the past, saying "good-bye."

February 14, 1944—Valentine's Day
Union Station, Los Angeles, California

"Come on, honey. I know it's hard. It's hard for me too," Lt. Neil Thomas said, tenderly holding Caroline's tearful face between his hands. By sheer fate, it was their first wedding anniversary, as well as the day that he was leaving for war.

Caroline tried to look happy, but it was no use. "I don't want you to go. I'm afraid, Neil. Hold me," she pleaded as they clung to each other.

The attendant was opening the metal doors at gates G and H leading into the tunnel. "First boarding call for Union Pacific Number 71, departing for San Francisco at track 12 in thirty minutes. Nonpassengers may accompany ticketed passengers to the tracks."

"Come on, Caroline. We'd better go," Neil prodded gently after the third call. Caroline tightened her grip on his arm, pressed against him even closer, but allowed him to lead her into the tunnel.

They walked along slowly with others, passing several boarding ramps to other tracks. The tunnel was overflowing with soldiers and their girls, an ocean of heartache in an uncertain future.

"The tunnel of love," Neil whispered in her ear. When Caroline raised her sad brown eyes to his, he pointed to the couples standing along the walls, kissing, repeating what he had just said. "The tunnel of love," he breathed, then pulled her to him in a long embrace.

"I love you," she said, laying her head against his chest.

"I love you, too," he whispered. He took her hand, then turned to face the tunnel. Moisture was welling in the corners of his eyes.

At the base of the long boarding ramp, Caroline stopped abruptly, suddenly feeling as though her legs were weighted to the floor.

"What's wrong, sweetheart?" he asked. "Are you afraid I can't fly well enough to get through this and come back to you?"

"No, it isn't that," she replied, fighting back the tears. She struggled to go on, but the words wouldn't come. Finally, almost inaudibly, she said, "I'm trying, Neil. I'm really trying. I'm just afraid that . . ."

They held on to each other at the foot of the concrete ramp as others passed by, oblivious, caught up in their own misery.

Caroline fought to regain control of her emotions, then finally gave voice to her fear. "I'm afraid if I let you go now, I'll never see you come back through this tunnel for me." She looked into his eyes, searching for some kind of assurance, a sign that her fears were imagined.

"I know," he said quietly. He gazed at her as if he were trying to imprint every detail, every feature of her face into his memory.

Seeing the pain in his eyes, Caroline knew he understood. She threw her arms around his neck and held him tighter than ever before.

"I've got to go, Caroline," he said sadly.

"Just one minute more," she pleaded, pulling herself out of his embrace. "I have something I want you to take with you." She reached into her bag, pulled out the envelope, then placed it in his hand. "It's a Valentine. For our anniversary. It's fragile. You'll need to take care of it."

Neil tore open the envelope and pulled out the card. Inside was a crushed red rose, a perfect rose from their garden. When he spoke again, his voice was choked with emotion. "I'll come back before next Valentine's Day, Caroline, I promise. I'll bring this back to you. Safe and sound. Just be here."

When Susan joined me in the kitchen a few minutes later, she sounded different, less sure of herself. The pages were still in her hand.

"I don't understand," she said.

"What's that?" I asked, pouring the coffee, trying to ignore the power of those questioning green eyes. "What is it you don't understand?"

"Your father and mother's anniversary was on Valentine's Day."

"Yes."

"He promised he'd return by the next Valentine's Day—so did he?"

I smiled. "You're just going to have to read the rest of the story."

She leaned back against the counter, crossing her arms thoughtfully. "They seem like genuinely warm people. I couldn't help seeing Donna Reed and Jimmy Stewart," she offered.

"I understand," I replied softly. "Around

here, they were a legend really. Why don't we take our coffee with us, and I'll show you around the place? My mother was very proud of her rose garden."

It had begun to rain. Susan was late for her plane. We'd lost track of time, talking for over an hour about the story, my mother's old stately Victorian home and her rose garden, and about ourselves. Susan seemed attentive to every detail of the house. I had showed her the photographs hanging on the walls, my mother's pictures, especially the one of my father in his uniform, aboard ship, holding the Valentine card in his hand that my mother had given him in the station. Susan studied the old photograph, but made no comment.

She finally agreed to read the story. When I handed it to her, she accepted it graciously, but tossed it into her leather attaché case and snapped it shut as if she were relieved to be locking it away. Now it was time for her to go.

We were standing at the base of the porch under the trellis in the rose garden. We'd met little more than an hour ago. Susan turned to look at me. She obviously had something to say.

"This house has a feeling to it. It feels—I don't know. Like there's a life to it." She seemed to be weighing her words. "It's a wonderful place. This probably sounds silly, but I can almost feel the love your mother put into it. What would you think about shooting the interview here? I mean, if you don't have to be out immediately."

I was surprised she'd felt the need to ask. "Of course," I said. "I own this house. I'm on no one's schedule but my own."

It was pouring now, but only a few drops of rain were filtering through the roses overhead, glistening on her dark silken hair and the soft skin of her face. She looked toward the bed of flowers along the drive.

"You must've been very happy growing up in this house," she said.

"We were. We were very happy."

Her next words seemed to tumble out. "This is the house I dreamed of as a little girl. When I first saw it, I could hardly believe my eyes." She stole a glance at my face. "When the pipes were leaking in our apartment, when we came home and found someone had picked the lock with a bobby pin, or when I watched my mother hang the same worn-out curtains in the new kitchen every time we moved, I'd climb under the covers at night to dream that we lived in a house just like this. A house with its own mailbox, its own front and backyard, its own flowers. This is that house." She stopped then and looked down at her keys.

I wasn't sure what to say. "I've decided to sell it. Too many ghosts here. Wonderful ghosts. Family ghosts. But ghosts just the same."

I had explained to her how my sweetheart Diane had died less than three years ago. I'd lost two of the most important people in my life, my mother and my wife, within twelve brutal months of each other. I hadn't talked to anyone about my feelings before, not even my children, but it had slipped out so easily in the last hour. "I guess I feel it's time to move on," I finished.

"I'm sorry," she said simply, then quickly changed the subject. "Listen, I've got some more research to do before we move on this. I'll need to contact Colonel

Jackson and set up an interview with him. I also want more details on the Japanese soldier's story. We have a bureau in Tokyo, but it's still going to take some time." She extended her hand. I took it. "I'll get back to you next Monday. My boss is really excited about this."

I nodded. She turned and ran for the car, holding her attaché case over her head against the rain. I stood transfixed for a moment, watching her move across the lawn. I caught up to her just as she opened the door.

"I guess you're anxious to get back and spend the weekend with your family," I ventured, holding the door open as she slid behind the wheel.

She popped the car in gear. "I guess if you call Daisy, my cat, family—then, yes," she said, and shut the door.

I stood in the rain with my hands in my pockets, feeling foolish, watching her back down the driveway, then onto Marengo Avenue. As she turned the corner, she waved. It was a small gesture, but I was grateful for it. I waved back.

A flicker of emotion went through me as I walked back to the house, a feeling I wasn't ready for. I consciously pushed it aside, and my thoughts went back, as always, to Diane. Everything here reminded me of her. We had spent twenty-five years together, working hard, striving to make something of our lives, watching our children grow. My parents had only one year together, but it had been enough to last a lifetime. So why was I feeling so empty now?

Oblivious to the rain, I walked along the side of the house to the porch steps, and ran my hand along the smooth stem of a budding rose. The barbs were still tender, not sharp as they soon would be. I frowned as the question resurfaced. Could I find a love again like I had known?

It was time to leave the thorns behind and reach for the new growth. I had allowed my todays to slip by one by one, unnoticed, as though they didn't exist. I was ready for a fresh start, in a place without roots, where the phantoms of the past would no longer haunt me. Even the specters of love are ghosts.

Driving back to the airport, Susan considered the man she'd just met, remembering the sincerity in his face as he told her about his story. A true believer, she thought.

She wasn't ready to admit to herself that the pages had filled her with an unfamiliar warmth, that she'd wanted to dive head-first into the world of Caroline and Lt. Thomas.

Pulling up to the Hertz office near LAX, Susan quickly pulled her thoughts back to the present. Within minutes, she had turned in the rental car, checked in at the gate, and was settling into a first-class seat on the plane, anxious to get back to work. Noticing only three or four other first-class passengers, she felt a sense of satisfaction in the fact that at age thirty-one, she'd earned her place with CNTV's *American Diary*. Her mother would've been proud.

Take care of yourself, her mother had always told her. Men can only be counted on to put themselves first, then abandon you. It was the lesson of Susan's childhood. Never rely on anyone else, especially a man, to get what you want in this world.

As the plane prepared for takeoff, its engines roaring, Susan opened her attaché case. It was going to be a long flight and she had plenty of work to do.

Neil Thomas's story was sitting on top. She gathered up the pages and looked at them. A strange sensation ran through her as she gazed upon his name. She stared into the page and couldn't help but recall the time she spent with him at the old home.

With a deep breath and a sigh, she began to read.

Roses Have Thorns

I will start at the beginning with a premise for a rare but true love story. The premise is this: All love stories weighted with tragedy possess equivalent hope for the opposite—triumph. As a pendulum may swing high in one direction, the laws of nature dictate that it must swing with equal force in the other. So it is with love. Love lost may yet be found, and love gained may yet experience loss.

But what are we to do? Should we never risk grabbing hold of love when it is presented before us? The poet

Tennyson said it best: " 'Tis better to have loved and lost, than never to have loved at all."

So I make this promise: I have written this story out of love, and have followed it from the perspectives of those who were a part of it. By telling it as it was passed along to me, through conversation, by reading my father's letters and the last Valentine, I offer here the dreams of one who first loved long ago, and lost, then triumphed in the end.

As you step back in time with Caroline, gaze at the world through her eyes, an aging woman who once dared to love, to hope, and to dream.

There are many kinds of love. Read between the lines and enjoy the journey. There are secrets waiting for you there. As the poet Moore said:

There's nothing half so sweet in life
As love's young dream.

Susan looked up from her reading. Her intellect was telling her to put the pages away, refuse the assignment, not get caught up in this fairy tale. The last thing she needed right now was to have her well-ordered life turned upside down by a romantic fantasy. She had allowed herself to believe in love once before, and she'd been deceived, just as her mother had been. But now Susan was in control of her life, and she had no intention of letting that slip away.

What was it about Neil, about his story, that was taking hold of her, sending her back to her childhood dreams? Was it the strangely familiar Victorian house, with its cardinal red roses, her favorite flower, or was it the warmth she'd seen in his sparkling blue eyes, the genuineness in his smile?

It was 5:30 P.M. The plane hadn't even taxied out of the terminal; yet Susan was already far away.

She was in her favorite hiding place, under a musty staircase in an apartment building on Boston's south side, where she'd lived with her mother as a child. The staircase had been her own private world, a place where she could close her eyes and transport herself away into her dreams.

A little girl's dreams. A Victorian house

in a tiny seaport town. Loving parents, playful children running happily along the seashore of Cape Elizabeth, a father who picked her up in his arms and hugged her close to him. A father who sat in his easy chair at night reading his newspaper, while she lay on the rug in front of the hearth, drawing pictures for him.

The announcement that the plane had been cleared for departure broke Susan's reverie. Within minutes, the jet was in the air. She looked down at the pages in her lap as the airplane swept over the bay, turning back toward the coastline on its course to Baltimore. She was headed back home, and somehow, she no longer felt like the same person she'd been when she left there days before.

By the time the plane reached cruising altitude, she had made a decision. She unfastened her seat belt, pulled a blanket and pillow out of the overhead compartment, and turned on the reading light. She began to read where she had left off.

"Roses have thorns." Words. Final words from the last letter my mother,

Caroline, received from my father Lt. Neil Thomas's battle station, aboard an aircraft carrier in the Pacific during World War II. A strange way to reassure her.

My mother understood the words though. She couldn't have known it then, but they would be the last words she would hear from him for fifty years . . . until the last Valentine.

It all ended in a strange way. Some would call it tragic. At worst, it was tragic. At best, it was an expression of a beauty rarely found, even in the most inspired and elevating music. The ending was both surprising and unexpected—melodious—like a crescendo and not a diminuendo. But then, surprise endings can be the most satisfying endings of all.

February 14, 1944—Valentine's Day
Union Station, Los Angeles, California

The conductor called for final boarding. Soldiers streamed by Caroline and Neil as they struggled to say their last good-bye.

"Caroline, you need to be brave for me, okay? Come on, baby." Neil was looking down at her as they stood below the steps of the last car on the train. She had worn his favorite dress, the red-and-white flowered one that showed off her curves so nicely.

"You're such a doll," he went on, then growled in her ear and nibbled it, which usually made her laugh. But she could only offer a weak smile.

"Come on, now," he prodded softly, lifting her chin up with his hand. "How could a guy get so lucky?" He kissed her on the forehead, wearing that smile she found so irresistible.

Caroline put her arms around his neck, searching his eyes. "I thought you didn't believe in luck."

"I said I didn't believe in bad luck when you don't have any luck at all. That only applies to marbles, crap shoots, and horseshoes. You're my luck, and I've felt that way since the first time you kissed me. The first time— back at Adams School. Remember?" When she smiled, tears rolling down her face, he pulled out a handkerchief.

"I almost forgot, I bought this for you on Olvera Street today. Look at the word embroidered in red. You minored in Spanish at City College. Let's see if you know what it means."

"*Felicidades.* It means—it means happiness to you," Caroline replied.

"See? What did I tell you! It's a sign of good luck. Look, it's got little patterns of flowers in the corners. Cute, don't you think?"

"Just like you," she said, trying her hardest to smile.

"That's my girl, Caroline."

The conductor's voice sounded again. "All aboard!"

They were running out of time. The crowd pulsed around them with final good-byes. The engines roared for departure.

He raised his voice above the noise. "I've loved you since Adams School, through the years in Eagle Rock, through all the good times, and I can't remember any bad. I think I've always loved you." He scooped her into his arms. They melted into one last embrace.

He stepped back to face her, then bent down to pick up his bag, which he'd dropped on the ground.

As he pulled away, he let go of her grasp. "No matter what happens, Caroline, I promise before God, I'll come back for you. We'll hold each other again right here! That's a promise."

"I'll be here waiting," she cried out as he stepped into the train.

He had to see her face one final time if he could. Throwing his bag on the seat next to a window, he flung it open and thrust his upper body outside, searching the crowd for her face.

The engines picked up steam. Caroline caught view of her man as she turned to leave. Running and breaking through the crowd, she reached for his arm as half his body reached out for her.

"I love you isn't good enough, darling. I'll return . . . I promise," he said, smothering her with his lips. They melted together in the struggle to kiss and embrace, until they couldn't any longer.

As the train pulled away, their hands

seemed linked through the space separating them. Like a photo aging before
her, he faded from view.

Caroline walked numbly up the tunnel
through the turnstile doors, passing
more soldiers and their sweethearts.
She knew they were feeling the same
pain, but it cut like a knife in her heart,
making her feel more alone.

Finding herself in the front lobby, she
headed outside.

"Read all about it! Marines take
Marianas Atoll! Seven thousand Japs
die! Americans land at Anzio," cried a
newsboy, hawking his papers on the
sidewalk.

The news sent a shiver up her spine.
Behind the words was the message
that American boys had also died. Silently, she cried out to God. "Protect
my sweetheart," she prayed. "Please
bring him back to me."

She found her way to their tan 1938
Ford V-8 sedan and put the keys in the
ignition. Leaning her head against the
steering wheel, she breathed deeply,

trying to control the feelings consuming her. She didn't care if anyone could see her, knowing they'd understand. There was heartache all around her.

But there was happiness, too. Boys who'd been gone for two years were rotating home, and it hurt to see their joy. Young girls were squealing in delight as they spotted their husbands or boyfriends.

She tried to gain the composure to drive the ten miles on the new Arroyo Seco Freeway back home to Pasadena. Sitting there, her light auburn hair brushing against the black leather seat, she wondered, *When did I start loving him?* The scene played out in her mind.

Eight-year-old Neil had asked, "Caroline, why did you kiss Richard yesterday over there, by the drinking fountain?"

"Like this?" Caroline answered. She giggled, kissing him on the cheek and hugging him tight. He tried to pull away, but they both lost their balance and sprawled to the ground. She found herself lying on top of him.

"Naughty girl!" scolded Miss Mc-Cullough. She leaned over and picked Caroline up by the arm, then marched her toward the office.

Neil, the new boy at school, had picked himself up and brushed off his clothes, ignoring the jeers of the other kids standing around.

She could still see him. The little boy in a red-and-white striped T-shirt, with holes in the knees of his jeans and silly suspenders. She smiled, remembering. He never needed them—his body was solid and slender—but he wore them until the navy made him take them off. He wanted to be like his dad.

Caroline remembered turning around as Miss McCullough opened the office door of the old country school, where she blew Neil a kiss.

The other children had hooted and howled, pushing him as they teased, "Neil has a girlfriend! Neil has a girl-friend!"

The poor kid, Caroline thought, turn-ing the key in the ignition. It would be a short trip back to Pasadena, but her heart would ache every mile.

"I Love You Isn't Good Enough"

Caroline pulled into the driveway of the white-frame Victorian sitting on an acre behind Marengo Avenue. They had purchased it in 1943, just one week after their marriage, when her uncle offered them a bargain they couldn't refuse. It was a wedding gift, of sorts. Built in the early 1900s, the house needed some work. One hundred dollars down payment, take over the monthly payments of fifty dollars, and continue paying until the five thousand still owed had been paid in full. The house, with four bedrooms upstairs, a living room down with kitchen, a mud room and surrounding porch, was all she had ever dreamed of.

She was home. She sat in the car, thinking how wonderful the past year had been. It had been a blessing to have him there, even though he was in the service. She stared at the house. She loved their "fixer-up mansion," as Neil liked to call it. It was a lovely yet suddenly lonely place. Now she was expecting their first child. She hoped that being occupied as a mother would help fill the empty space. She wondered how it could.

She had loved to see Neil there. He would smile as he worked up a sweat, whistling a tune or imitating Frank Sinatra as they worked on each room of the house, sanding, painting, turning it into a place to be proud of. His navy assignment as a flight training officer at the Santa Monica and Long Beach airfields was almost too good to be true. He was home most nights, but serving the war effort at the same time. Deep down inside, she'd always known it was too good to be true—too good to last. But she'd refused to believe.

She thought about the hand-carved sign Neil had hung over the entry on the inside of the front door. She could still hear him driving a nail through its center, then calling her over to see what he'd done.

"Caroline, come see if this thing is level." He was standing on an old wooden stepladder.

"Neil, where did you get that? I love it!"

"An old-timer friend of mine from the train station carved it. He used to work for my dad in the shipping department. Does it look level to you?"

"Not only level, but well thought out. Did you think that up or did someone else say it?" Caroline laughed.

"It was my idea to hang it over the door, but it was my mother's favorite quote. Some guy named Paul from the New Testament," Neil responded through his teeth, two nails hanging be-tween his lips.

"Belief is the substance of things hoped for, the evidence of things not seen," Caroline read as he finished nailing the small sign into place.

He stood back to inspect it. "Yep. Level the first time. Belief, Caroline. That's all you need. Then, as you work for it, the miracle happens like magic. Just like the blueprint your uncle followed to build this house—" As he turned toward her, her arms went around his neck, and her lips met his in a kiss.

"See? Just like I said, the substance of things hoped for," he laughed. "Turn out the lights, chicken. It's time to hit the sack."

In just one year, he had been called up. Caroline's eyes roamed the front of the house and the porch as she sat daydreaming in the car. She thought about all the nights he was home. They'd had a warm beginning. No one could have been better for her than Neil.

When he came home from the airfield in the evenings, they'd sit on the porch swing, holding each other, staring at the San Gabriel Mountains and the star-filled sky as they talked. Some-times they'd play records on the old Victrola or listen to the Philco broad-casts of Radio City Music Hall, and the war would seem a million miles away.

Then the news would come on the radio. Neil would be suddenly alert, anxious, all of his attention focused on the events taking place on the battle-fronts. Caroline knew what he was thinking. That he should be there, not here, with his cushy flight-training job that allowed him to go home to his wife three, even four times a week. He was cheating death without honor. It was written all over his face each time the news came on.

Some of the neighbors made her aware of it, too. They'd comment on how nice it must be to have her hus-band safely at home while their hus-bands or sons were risking their lives overseas.

Caroline sat in the car, caught up in the visions of how it had been. An empty house awaited her, and she wanted to stay in the past, in the year that her dreams began to take shape—

those "things hoped for." She pulled out the handkerchief he'd given her just hours before, stared at the word in her hands. A smile came to her face as a memory flashed through her mind.

It had been one year earlier, January 30, 1943, that she'd found the love she thought she had lost. It had been six years since she'd seen him. She had been, that day, one of three USO girls serving free coffee and donuts to servicemen at Union Station, the place where they'd just now said their good-byes.

Twenty-four-year-old navy lieutenant Neil Thomas was arriving back home in LA. It had been six long years since his father was transferred by Union Pacific Railroad to the Ogden, Utah, station. The country was in the midst of a depression. The Thomas family didn't want to leave Los Angeles, but it was take the transfer or lose the job. They'd moved to Ogden. He thought about all that had happened since he'd been gone, how fate had had its way with him.

Walking down the wooden ramp, he'd entered the tunnel leading under the tracks and into the main waiting area. It was packed with servicemen, most of them shipping out to the fronts. Here he was, being shipped out to Long Beach to flight-training school as an instructor. He never dreamed that he'd be assigned state-side duty during the biggest war the world had known, and it bothered him. He'd be training other men to fight, maybe die, in his place. Both of his brothers had been shipped overseas, and Billy. He shook his head and sighed.

Neil wasn't sure what to do with his two-week pass. His Uncle John still lived in Santa Monica, and he knew he'd be welcome there. Perhaps he could borrow the car and visit his old friends in Eagle Rock and Pasadena, if any of them were still around.

His bags bumped against other people, but no one seemed to notice. The station was crowded, and everyone had too much on their minds. Most of the guys had girls hanging on their arms, making him feel even worse.

Passing through the turnstile at gate H, he entered the main lobby and noticed the room. Last time he'd seen it, the station was still under construction. The lobby had a high wood-beamed ceiling, with mosaic tiles surrounding the walls and covering the floors. The handrails and doorknobs were brass, and the chairs and benches were covered in leather. Los Angeles. A pure class act.

Neil noticed the USO tables, where the pretty young women were serving the soldiers. He was in no hurry to go anywhere. Coffee, donuts, and a little conversation sounded perfect right now.

He moved to the back of the line, trying to get a look at the women at the table, but a group of noisy, raucous sailors was blocking the way. He cleared his throat loudly.

"What's your name, sailor?" he said, tapping one of them on the back.

The young man turned around slowly, as if ready to fight, but quickly saluted at the sight of Neil's uniform. "Peterson, sir."

"Peterson, are you coming in to LA or shipping out?" Neil asked in a commanding tone.

"Shipping out, sir."

"Quite a group of you here. All on the same ship assignment?"

"Yeah. I mean . . . yes, sir."

"I just heard the boarding calls have been changed on one of the trains heading out. Looks like it's leaving at track eleven in a few minutes. What's your train number?"

"Forty-nine, sir."

"Well, sailor, I think you're missing your train. I sure wouldn't want to be missing my ship. Would you?"

"No, *sir*. Hey, fellas, this officer says our number's been called. Departure time was changed. Come on."

The group grumbled, grabbing extra donuts as they left. Neil moved up to the table.

One young woman was serving. The other two were looking for something on the floor. His eyes were drawn to one of them immediately. Even with her head down, he could see she was attractive, and her profile was familiar.

He wasn't sure why his heart was suddenly pounding but decided to find out. He stepped around the table to offer his help.

"What can I do for you?" asked the brunette without looking up.

He couldn't help noticing her petite figure. The top of her blue blouse was unbuttoned, revealing more than she probably intended.

Neil cleared his throat. "Uh, hum, I wondered if I could be of any help," he said.

She straightened and quickly put a hand to her blouse, clearly annoyed. But her expression changed instantly when she looked at his face. She gasped, covering her mouth with her free hand.

"It can't be—you're not—" she stuttered, backing away, her hand still clinging to her blouse.

Neil smiled. He couldn't believe his luck. Maybe there was a God after all.

"Caroline. Caroline Jensen? I mean, Caroline Terry? What are you doing here? I heard you got married."

Neil took off his officer's cap, revealing his wavy black hair in a military cut. He stood waiting, offering his boyish grin.

"Neil? It can't be!" Both hands flew to her mouth. "I thought you were dead, that you were killed over Europe in a bombing raid. Is it really you?" she said, a thousand questions in her eyes.

"It's me, Caroline. I'm alive," he said, his voice soft, reassuring. "It was my brother—Billy. He was killed in a B-17 raid two months ago." His voice brightened. "Hey! How about a hug for a resurrected dead man?" He held his arms out to her. He had been in love with her once, and the years that had separated them seemed to be melting away.

"Oh, Neil!" She threw herself into his arms. As they held each other for a long happy moment, the soldiers waiting in line cheered, helping themselves to donuts and coffee. One of the girls whispered to the other as if she understood what had happened.

"By the way, I didn't get married," Caroline said, pulling herself from his arms. She looked into his eyes, asking, "But, Neil, how—?"

Animated, he leaned over and kissed her gently on the cheek. "Got orders for state-side duty. I'm a pilot, a navy flight-training officer. I'm going to be working with pilot trainees at the new schools opening up in Long Beach and Santa Monica." Neil suddenly didn't feel so bad about missing the war action. He was feeling seventeen again.

"I'm shocked, Neil! Stunned! You'll have to forgive me," she said, turning to one of the other girls, her sister, who was happily taking in the drama. "Jenny, it's Neil. Neil Thomas."

"Yeah, I can see that," Jenny replied, grinning. "It's so good to see you, Neil." She walked up to him and gave him a warm embrace. "You look—well, so good!" She stepped back and turned to Caroline, then whispered, "My gosh, he's handsome! You'd better not lose him this time. You do, and I'll be after him."

Caroline nudged her sister on the shoulder and wiped away the moisture in her eyes. The shock on her face had become a welcoming smile.

"Hey, I'm kinda hungry, and donuts won't do the trick. Jenny?" Neil said.

"Sure. You two go get reacquainted. Sally and I will be fine here. Besides, these guys seem to be helping themselves anyway," she laughed. The other girl nodded, winking at Caroline.

"Thanks, guys!" she said. Caroline grabbed Neil's arm and asked, "Where to?"

"Mexican food sound okay, across Alameda at Olvera Street? It's been a long time since I've had any LA-style Mexican cuisine. Utah hasn't discovered it yet."

"Sounds good to me. I've got a favorite place over there."

"Are my bags okay here for a while, Jenny?" he asked.

"Sure, just scoot 'em under the table there," she said, gesturing with her elbow as she began pouring coffee.

"Thanks," he said, then smiled as he turned to escort Caroline out of the station.

"I can't tell you what this means to have you with me. I was kind of down, but seeing you again—well, I guess we have a lot to catch up on, with me being dead and all," he laughed nervously.

"Yes, I think we do." She held his arm close as they exited through the front doors to Alameda Street and the place called "Pueblo de Los Angeles," Olvera Street. "I've never quit thinking about you, Neil," she added softly as they walked along.

Neil looked down at her, feeling an urge to say it, the words he'd blurted out years ago at the Rose Parade when they'd gone on a date, their last one before he moved. He stopped her on the sidewalk leading to Alameda Street.

"I feel like a kid again, and I wasn't very shy as a kid, was I?" He smiled, searching her eyes for a spark of memory. Her facial expression said everything as she gave him a wide smile.

"Remember the words I spit out that day long ago, at the Rose Parade? It was the last one we went to together. We were still in our teens. Remember what I said?"

"Yes," she whispered as she drew closer to him.

"I've felt that way about you since grade school, Caroline," he said tenderly, wanting to reach out to her, hold her.

"Say them again, Neil," she responded, a smile creasing the soft skin of her face as she closed her eyes.

"I love you isn't good enough. Not for you, Caroline."

He held her by the waist as they stood on the sidewalk. Her eyes and her smile revealed her thoughts to him. Slowly, carefully, he moved his lips toward hers.

Caroline welcomed him home.

Back in Pasadena, Caroline sat in her car for at least half an hour, remembering how she'd found Neil in the train station that day, one year before.

Memories. She had just seen him off to war. Now she was facing an uncertain future. Memories of being so in love, with nothing interrupting its flow. A mixed blessing, she thought. That was one year before. One year and two weeks before today.

Today was their first wedding anniversary, February 14, 1944. Today she'd tearfully said good-bye to him at that same place. Today he'd got his manly wish, to go off to war. She hit the steering wheel with her hand as she sat there in the driveway of their home, not wanting to go inside. She was alone and feeling empty as she sat there, thinking, remembering. Memories could be so sweet—and now?

The memory that had replayed in her mind weighed on her now. She stepped out of the car to see something lying on the driveway. Bending over to pick it up, she saw it was a copy of a picture, a wedding photo taken one year earlier. She was in her wedding gown, Neil dressed in his navy officer white dress uniform.

Finding it there sent a chill through her body. Bad luck! The thought came suddenly. "No, just silly superstition," she voiced, trying to convince herself by mumbling the words out loud. She fought to put it out of her mind as she walked up to the porch, staring at the photograph intently, wondering how it had gotten there. The last time she'd seen it, it was with the others she was arranging for the family album. Maybe Neil had picked it up, meaning to take it with him, and it had dropped out of his hand somehow.

She was glad she had found it. Turning it over, she noticed his writing. "Lt. Neil Thomas and Caroline Jensen Thomas, husband and wife—forever. February 14th, 1943." It brought a smile to her face, a face that had so recently been covered in tears. She was glad to be home, safe, even if he couldn't be there. Just moments before, she hadn't wanted to go into her empty "mansion." Now she couldn't control the roller coaster of emotions she felt.

She opened the screen door, fumbling with her keys as she unlocked the solid oak raised-panel door with the small window in the center. The window was at eye level, letting light into the entry hall with its small coat closet and mail drop. She took off her coat and hung it there.

Picking up the mail from the box, she found a letter from Neil. She hurried into the living room, set her purse down on the end table, and fell back into the cushioned sofa. Anxiously, she opened it, thinking he must have slipped it into the box as they left the house.

Feb. 14, 1944
Dearest Caroline,

It's hard for me to leave you, especially on this day, our wedding anniversary. You know that I felt it was my duty to volunteer. I couldn't keep sending other guys off to fight, maybe die, without guilt hitting me hard. I would never leave you. But so many are in the same boat we are. Please understand. I love you. It will all work out right.

Bing Crosby says it better, in that song you and I danced to as we listened to the radio last night.

Because you speak to me, I find
the roses 'round my feet,

*and I am left with tears and joy of
    thee.
Because God made thee mine, I'll
    cherish thee,
through all life and darkness and
    all time to be.*

*And pray His love may make our
    love divine.
Because God made thee mine!*

I left you a fresh rose by the bed on
the nightstand before leaving today. I
even wrote an original poem. Not as
elegant as Bing's verses, maybe even
silly, but I like to think of you smiling,
so here goes:

*Roses are red, violets are blue,
This poem isn't perfect, but my
    love is for you.
The flower I leave with the card,
    here behind,
is a symbol of beauty, a picture of
    mind.
And the picture I'll hold in my
    thoughts are of those . . .*

> *your face, your love, and this*
>   *symbol—the rose!*

> *I love you isn't good enough. Not for*
> *you, Caroline. I'll come back, you'll*
> *see. I'll be your last valentine. Forever*
> *is a promise to keep.*
>   *Your loving husband,*
>   *Neil*

She could still feel him close as she held the card to her breast. She leaned back in the sofa, her eyes closed. Even the smell of the greasy clothes thrown on the floor of the laundry room was evidence that he had been there just hours before. He had used the overalls to tune up the car once more. "Good enough to last one full year," he had said.

She got up, weary from the anxiety of making the last few hours with him meaningful. Entering the small main floor study, she gazed out the bay window to the rose garden they had planted together, then walked up the stairs to their room.

She turned toward the dresser. The smell of his aftershave still lingered in the room. Old Spice. She went over to the white cologne bottle with a sailing ship on it, uncorked it, holding it to her nose with her eyes closed. It was as if he were still here. It smelled like him—clean, smiling, holding her in his arms. Neil.

Hearing the unmistakable roar of B-29 Superfortresses flying overhead, she put the bottle down and peered out the window. They were heading north-west, probably to the Burbank Army Airfield, she thought. As she watched them disappear over the hills that created Arroyo Seco and surrounded the Rose Bowl, she thought about Neil's excitement to fly.

He was looking forward to a career after the war. "Aviation is the future," he'd say.

Once the planes had passed out of sight, she looked back to the roses. Spring was just around the corner, and the first hints of leaves and buds were showing. It had made perfect sense to her when Neil had suggested it. A rose garden, some gardenias, carnations, and chrysanthemums. Gradually, as they'd cultivated them, his plan to sell them each year to Rose Parade float designers could indeed pay off. He called it their "retirement account." He had put a lot of care and love into those first roses.

She filled her lungs with a breath of the fresh, springlike air that had entered the empty house, then laid the card down on the nightstand next to the poster bed and picked up the single-stem rose. Inhaling its fragrance, she left the room to wander outdoors.

More planes appeared, high overhead. The gentle noise of war, she whispered. It never seems to end.

The engines weren't frightening, but comforting. Perhaps because they were friendly sounds, sounds of an entire nation gearing up, turning out equipment and machines. Everyone seemed to have something to do behind the scenes for the war effort. They planted victory gardens, collected scrap metal and rubber for recycling;

everyone was united, bound together in a sense of patriotism. The ugliness of war was distant, only coming too close on the theater screen.

You could go down to the cinema, the Jensen Theater on Raymond Street, where the latest film clips from the battlefronts would be shown every Saturday. But it all seemed so far away, and the patriotic sounds and music behind the announcer's commanding voice made it feel somehow right, as if the war were a good cause, as if this were a good war. The boys would be marching home soon, with their proud tokens of battle, standing erect as they filed shoulder to shoulder, victorious. After all was said and done, all would be right with the world.

Looking up at the war planes, it was hard for Caroline to envision them being used in desperate attempts to kill other people in anger. Neil killing in anger, others trying to kill him. The thought made her shudder.

Her eyes returned to the rose garden. They'd be blossoming soon. She whispered, "Every rose, every carefully planted flower will remind me of him." She took another deep breath, then walked back to the house to pray.

La Golondrina

It was evening. Caroline sat in the living room, waiting for her sister, Jenny, to arrive. She had a fire going and had turned the small table-size Philco radio on. Dialing the tuner, she found the CBS Radio Network. The music made her smile. She was listening to the broadcasts from Radio City Music Hall in New York, one of the songs reminding her of their honeymoon. She remembered the hotel, the beach near Santa Monica, as the announcer presented Capt. Glenn Miller and his Army Air Corps Orchestra.

Caroline sat curled up on the sofa, holding a pillow to her as she stared into the glowing fire, listening.

She wondered how long, how many days or months it would take before missing him got any easier. The songs continued when she heard the knock at the door.

"Hi, doll face!" Jenny said, peering through the small window.

"I'm glad you're here," Caroline said, hurriedly opening the door to give her older sister a hug. "I need someone to talk to."

Jenny hung her coat in the hall closet, then followed Caroline to the sofa near the fireplace. After a brief silence, with the radio down low, she finally urged her sister on.

"How'd it go today, Sis? I mean, what did you do before seeing Neil off? I know it must've been hard," she offered in a soft, comforting tone.

Caroline tilted her head back and stared at the ceiling, searching. "Yeah, real hard," came her reply with a sigh. "Oh, Jenny, it's got me so scared. I'm afraid—afraid he won't be coming back. I keep thinking about Tommy Jones, Phil Johnson, Neil's brother— some of the other boys who've been killed, and it's got me scared."

Jenny drew herself closer and put her arms around her younger sister. It wasn't realistic to say she knew he'd be coming home, but she had to re-assure Caroline. "Hey, sweetheart, come on now. He'll be okay, you'll see. He's a top flight trainer, he's tough, and he's smart."

Caroline looked up at her sister, im-ploring. "He may be Superman to me, but he can't stop bullets. He can't stop bullets, Jenny." She looked at her sis-ter, wanting her to tell her she was wrong, that he *could* stop bullets.

There was nothing Jenny could say to comfort her. "It'll be all right," she tried. "You'll see, Sis."

They sat there, the music washing over them. Caroline gradually com-posed herself and they started to talk.

"It's normal, the way you feel," Jenny said. "You're afraid. We're all afraid. The best thing to do is write letters, send things, and plan for the future. If you plan for the future, then you have hope. You can live in the past, Sis, when you want to be alone with him, but look to the future. See him coming back to you, there at the station. Remember what Mom always told us before we went to bed?"

"Yeah," she replied, and they voiced it together.

" 'Don't forget to say your prayers, girls.' " They were holding hands, both smiling as Caroline wiped away the last tears staining her face.

"That's what's holding me together, I think." It was more than words to Caroline. It was her lifeline.

A quiet moment followed as they listened to the radio, which was still turned down low. The crooner, Frank Sinatra, was singing. Jenny decided to try to get Caroline to open up.

"So tell me about today. What did you do before Neil boarded the train? Did you go out or something?"

"We had a good time," she responded in a quiet tone as she moved to the hearth, adding a small log to the fire. "We walked around town for a while. We went up to Chinatown, then back to Olvera Street. You know, the place across from Union Station with all those souvenir shops. We had lunch at La Golondrina Restaurant, where Neil gave me the ring about a year ago. The old Catholic church built in the late seventeen hundreds was open. Neil stopped there and asked me if I wanted to join him, to go inside and pray. I shook my head and left him alone for a few minutes. When he came back out, we bought some souvenirs and I tried out my Spanish. It was fun."

Without knowing she'd done it, Caroline had pulled out the handkerchief. She was twisting it in her hands as she stared at the fire, remembering the afternoon. Her sister sat quietly.

"He gave me this," she said, showing it to Jenny. As she said it, she realized that Neil wanted her to be happy. She had to try.

"Oh, Jenny, you've got to hear this. We were sitting in La Golondrina, waiting for our order to arrive. The mariachis were playing. Neil got up and took my hand, leading me out to the dance floor. He started to dance, trying to cha-cha or rumba or something like that. He had me in hysterics. People started to clap and whistle. Pretty soon every sailor, marine, and soldier who could find a girl was up and dancing. The rest sat there, cheering and clapping to the rhythm."

"Neil. Always the life of the party," laughed Jenny.

Caroline continued, "Neil had a Mexican sombrero on his head. I guess I really got into it then. I started stomping my feet, and some sailors started whistling, which egged me on even more. I really didn't want the day to be all doom and gloom. Then I did that thing with my skirt—you know, the way the Mexican girls do when they're dancing, flinging it around from side to side.

"The sailors started yelling, 'Go, Lieutenant! Kiss her,' and the whole place chimed in as they clapped. Neil finally gave in, leaning me back first, like they do in the movies. They all whistled and clapped. Soon guys were kissing girls all over the place. It was a riot. We left the dance floor laughing so hard, tears flowed. After we finished our meal, we went to the station."

Jenny was enjoying the laughter, the light side she was seeing in Caroline. They talked for hours after that about the old gang and growing up in Eagle Rock. Eventually, the conversation turned to the yearly trek the Jensen and Thomas families made to the Rose Parade with a few other friends, turning it into a tradition.

"Remember the parade in thirty-seven—or was it thirty-eight?"

"It was thirty-seven," Caroline said with a smile. "The month before Neil moved away with his family. For all of those years, I had such a crush on him, and I finally found out that day how he felt about me."

Since childhood, Caroline, Neil, their brothers and sisters, and hundreds of thousands of others had lined the route of the famous Rose Parade in Pasadena. The tradition had started in 1933. The families would find a spot on Colorado Boulevard the day before and camp out, then start celebrating.

On Raymond Street, the bells of Saint Andrew's Cathedral would ring out at midnight. When they sounded, the street would burst into sound. Horns honking, firecrackers exploding, party whistles blowing. Sometimes a few cars would get together and turn up a radio station that was bringing in the New Year with the hits of the year before.

Colorado Boulevard and Raymond Street made up a prime corner—within short walking or running distance, depending on the need, to Saint Andrew's, where Neil and his family attended mass. The church had one of the most important features for a long evening of partying—restrooms, made available to the public.

Also on Raymond, just two short blocks south of Saint Andrew's, was the Jensen Theater, built in the 1920s. Although it belonged to a distant relative, it carried her name. In Caroline's mind the street was theirs.

She remembered the first time, at that Rose Parade, when she'd first thought she had noticed him noticing her. Soon they were making eyes and teasing each other. She was sure Neil knew how she felt about him. She had given him plenty of hints.

On that 1937 Rose Parade Eve, the gang was huddled closely together. The boys had stoked a fire in a trash can and they were singing songs, but it was cold, and Caroline couldn't stop shivering.

They all had blankets, but Neil must have noticed hers wasn't enough. He brought his over, putting it over her shoulders. He stood back then, and warmed his hands over the fire with the other boys, who were laughing and cracking jokes. Caroline remembered smiling appreciatively, then suddenly sensing something different about him. He kept glancing her way, as if checking on her.

She wanted to make sure he knew how she felt. She decided to risk it all on his next glance. "Thank you, Neil," she whispered, then added, "I love you," mouthed in silence.

He stood, staring back at her. Then he blurted the precious words that would become the refrain of their grow-ing love. "I love you isn't good enough. Not for you, Caroline!"

His brother Bill, who was laughing it up with their brother Johnny and Car-oline's brother Pete, caught Neil's look and heard what he said. He teased his brother unmercifully by chanting the ro-mantic remark.

Neil had finally had enough. Instead of striking back, though, he sat down next to Caroline and pulled a part of the blanket over his shoulders to share it with her. He turned to her and winked, then reached for her hand.

There was silence for a minute. Neil's brothers had expected him to fight back or leave, escape the ha-rassment. But he put his arm around Caroline. She snuggled up to him un-abashedly in front of their families.

With morning came an event that would make that Rose Parade even more memorable. As it began, and the queen's float passed by, a bouquet of roses bordering the stand on her float fell to the ground near the group. See-ing a mounted policeman's horse was about to crush the roses under its feet, Neil ran out and grabbed them. Returning to stand in front of Caroline, who was cheering along with the other onlookers at his rescue, he bowed before her, then went down on one knee and handed her the bouquet. The crowd cheered louder. A photographer from the *Los Angeles Gazette* caught the scene as the mounted policeman stopped his horse in front of them. Neil announced, "For a true Rose Queen," and the crowd roared its approval. The newspaper reported the scene, with the caption, "Rescue of the Roses! Gentleman of the Court Honors a Rose Parade Queen."

The glass-enclosed photograph of that New Year's Day event graced the mantle over the small stone hearth of their fireplace. Jenny laughed with her sister as they relived that and the other New Year's days they had spent together on Colorado Boulevard.

"How about some coffee and donuts? I made them fresh this afternoon," Caroline said, standing up.

"Sure, Sis. Anything'll be fine," Jenny said, following her into the kitchen.

"I wish we could go back to those days, Jenny, but it all ended with the attack on Pearl Harbor. And it was never the same after Neil moved to Utah," she said as she poured the coffee, placing it on a tray with the donuts.

As they returned to the living room, Jenny said, "Sis, what do you think you'd be doing right now if you hadn't been at the USO table in the train station last year?"

"What do you mean, Jenny?"

"You know, if you and I hadn't filled in for Mary and her partner. What are the chances that you would have gotten a marriage proposal that day?"

Caroline smiled. "I guess there is justice in the universe, isn't there? There is a God."

"See! You're happy just thinking about it. The risk of marrying a man who you knew could be shipped off to war was worth it, wasn't it?"

"Yeah," Caroline agreed, biting into a donut.

"So answer my question. What

would you be doing right now, this year, if you and Neil hadn't found each other again? You know. He would have thought you married Fred Terry, and you'd probably still think he was dead."

"I never thought much about it," she replied. "I just assumed it was the hand of God in our lives, that it was destined to happen. To meet him again," Caroline answered. They were silent for a moment, a warmth in their moods that was missing before. It was getting late, but Jenny was staying the night.

"So before you saw Neil off today," she began, "you had lunch at the restaurant he proposed to you in. What's the name—La Goldrina? La Golrina?"

"La Gol-on-drina," Caroline said, pronouncing each syllable slowly for her sister.

"La Gol-on-drina," Jenny repeated. "What does it mean? Is it food or something?" She laughed at her own remark.

The question made Caroline remember what she'd seen in the window that day. A small bird. A robin, a sparrow, or—a shiver ran up her spine, catching her off guard. Her mind went back to another day, a year earlier.

She had been picking up a few things for a birthday party at the market near her mother's home in Eagle Rock, when she ran into an old friend. Her friend told her a swallow had shown up one day on the kitchen windowsill while she was doing dishes, and that it just sat there. She broke down and cried as she told Caroline that a Western Union telegram arrived three days later. Her brother had died the same day the swallow appeared, killed in action on Guadalcanal.

"Superstition. Silly superstition," Caroline muttered, folding her arms over her body, fighting the chill.

"Caroline, you're cold! You have goose bumps. Honey, what's wrong?" Jenny asked, moving closer to rub her sister's arms.

Caroline turned to her sister, trying to suppress her sudden fear. "Swallow," she said. "*Golondrina* means 'swallow' in Spanish."

February 14, 1994—11:30 A.M.
Union Station Lobby, Los Angeles,
California

"Who's the old lady?" the custodian Armando asked his friend, motioning toward Caroline, who was sitting in the waiting station chair.

"That, my good man, is none other than Mrs. Caroline Jensen Thomas. She's a regular here. Like clockwork. I can always tell when it's February 14th, even if I don't have a calendar. Come Valentine's Day, she'll be here, no questions asked," answered Josiah Williams, the Union Station security guard. "We been good friends twenty-five years now. I kinda watch over her, wake her up a few times, just in case, makin' sure she's okay. She's one fine lady, I tell you that, Mando, a real sweetheart, yes sirree." Josiah reached over and tapped the old woman on the shoulder as Armando swept the polished tile floor of the old train station lobby.

"Miss Caroline—you okay, sweetheart? Miss Caroline?" Josiah shook her gently to let her know he was there.

She slowly opened her eyes and reached for the glasses she had set on her lap. Struggling to put them on, she finally focused as she looked up at her Union Station guardian.

"Oh, Josiah. I'm so glad you're here. For a minute, I thought it was Neil coming to get me." She dropped her brown eyes in confusion mixed with embarrassment.

Josiah chuckled. "I understand, Miss Caroline. It's just old Josiah, makin' sure you're okay. I'm glad to see you're still gettin' down here, little lady. Another year gone by, and you're still comin', for how many years now, honey?"

"Fifty years since I last saw him. I've come for fifty years, including Valentine's Day 1944. It seems like yesterday. This place doesn't change, Josiah. Come sit with me, won't you?" she replied, weakly patting the empty seat beside her.

Josiah knew he shouldn't take the time, but seniority did have its privileges. Besides, he thought, he could chalk it up to public relations. "Sure, little lady. Why sure. I'd like to take a minute," he answered, sitting down.

"You know, this makes twenty-five years since I started workin' here, Miss Caroline. You remember the first time I caught you sleepin' here on the bench, and I thought you was some sort of bag lady?" Josiah laughed loudly, then went on, "You was the prettiest old bag lady I ever seen though, and I was determined to do my job. You really straightened young Josiah out, didn't you, honey?"

Caroline's lined face broke into a wide grin. "Pretty fancy dresser for an old bag lady, and pretty good with this walking stick," she said, raising her cane toward him as he pretended to block it. "I guess you startled me. I was too quick with my cane, but it was good training for a new security man, right, Josiah?"

She was so happy to see her old friend. He had been so comforting during all those visits, year after year. He had watched out for her. He had come to work at Union Station back in 1970, when she had just turned fifty years old. Hardly an old bag lady.

Josiah relaxed a bit as he sat next to her. He reached over to take her slightly trembling hand from the arm-rest. He turned toward her, cupping one hand gently over hers, then reached over to give her a kiss on the forehead.

"Thank you, Caroline. Thank you for what you did for me and my Martha. If it hadn't been for you—well, she's dealin' real well with our boy Charlie dyin' over there in Vietnam. I tell you this every year, don't I, honey?"

She looked up at him with compassion in her eyes, simply answering, "Yes." Her voice had aged gracefully. It was slower and shaky, but each word was soft, deliberate.

"You remember me tryin' to help you, and then feelin' that you'd been the one helpin' me?" he asked.

Caroline looked at him with a smile on her lips and a gleam in her eyes. She nodded in reply.

"I wasn't sure what to make of you," Josiah continued. "Then you got up and walked over to McCarthy's Café, and told me to follow you. You waved me over to a table; and just when I thought I was gonna have to listen to an old crazy woman talkin', you told me to sit down."

"I told you to sit down and be quiet," she corrected.

"I was just gettin' to that," he laughed. "Then you told me to take a break, and you bought me a cup of coffee. I'll never forget how it hit me when you said you wanted to tell me some history, a war story. It had been just three weeks since our Charlie'd been killed."

"I didn't know about the loss of your son, Josiah. I felt so bad when you told me," she replied.

"How could you know, Miss Caroline? You know, what you said made so much sense, about your husband being lost over the Philippines during World War II and all. How you knew he was probably dead, even though he'd been officially declared missing in action. Well, it sure did help to see how someone who lost a loved one was behaving, you taking life with a smile and a song and all. And then you said, 'Josiah, as long as love is alive, the dead never die. It's not in the end alone that we love, but along the way. A love that endures the thorns of life calls out to us. When we listen, it lights the ground on which we walk and we know that we're not alone. And when the flame of life flickers out and is no more, the love you showed to others will light the ground for them to walk upon.' "

"Josiah, you're eloquent! Did I say that?"

"You sure did. You wrote it down, and I've been sharing it with others all these years."

"I see," Caroline said with quiet humility.

After a moment of silence, Josiah added, "He was a special boy, my boy Charlie was. Now, 'cause you helped show us how we could handle it, we got dozens of kids calling us Mom and Pop. That was real good of you, teaching Martha how to reach out and lose herself like that. She sees a hurt in other people's lives, and she's there for them." A hint of tears came to his eyes as he looked away. He cleared his throat. "She's been a real good teacher too. Just like you, sweetie." He leaned over to give her another kiss on the forehead as he stood up to leave.

"I remember talking to you, then having dinner with you and Martha, but my mind—sometimes I think I leave it at home," Caroline said, looking at him with questioning eyes. "I'm having trouble remembering a lot of things these days, Josiah." She brightened then. "I wish I could go see Martha one more time. Tell her I said I love her, and that I'm proud of her, will you?" Her voice was imploring, soft, and gentle.

Josiah could see how tired she was. It worried him. "Yes, ma'am, but what do you mean, you wish you could see her one more time? Miss Caroline, you're invited any ol' time. You going somewhere, moving maybe?"

"No, not from here anyway, Josiah," she said, fumbling with the fifty-year-old letter in her lap. "This is from my Neil. The navy brought it to me. He's coming to get me and take me home today." She gestured weakly with her hands to the old card, trying to pick it up in her trembling hands.

Josiah, standing up to position himself in front of her, knelt down to look her in the eyes. "You don't mean your husband, Neil. You mean Neil Junior, don't you now, Caroline." It wasn't a question.

"No, Josiah. Neil Junior is with my grandson Eric at his basketball game. He won't be coming to take me home. Lt. Neil Thomas is coming today. I know he will." She stared off toward the windows and the old wall clock hanging over the doors to the patio on the south side of the waiting area. She seemed to be watching the birds at play.

He followed her eyes. "What are you lookin' at, honey?"

"Las golondrinas," she whispered, a smile on her face.

Susan and Neil

Wednesday, January 14, 1998
Baltimore, Maryland

It had been five days since Susan's meeting with Neil in Pasadena. Since then, she hadn't been able to get him, or his story, off her mind; but the frenzied pace that greeted her when she got back to the office had kept her from reading beyond the first half. What she had read had been enough, though, to tell her she wanted to do this interview. She was hooked.

Craig Warren hadn't bothered to tell her

until she got back that he'd scheduled the story to air on February 14th, if they decided to do it, as a Valentine's Day special. Only four weeks away. She'd fought him at first, arguing that she needed at least sixty days to get a show like this together, but she'd finally agreed to take on the challenge. It was, after all, a brilliant idea.

By the time she got back to Baltimore on Friday and put the pages of Neil's story back in her attaché case, she was beginning to resent the pace she normally thrived on. It was keeping her from reading, forcing her to focus on the mechanics of doing the interview, when all she really wanted to do was bury herself in the past, lose herself in the story of Caroline and Lieutenant Thomas's 1940s wartime romance.

She checked the clock on the control room wall across from her desk. It was 10:00 A.M. She'd had at least five cups of coffee already, checking the clock every few minutes, struggling to concentrate on digging her way out of the mounting pile of paperwork on her desk. She was already two days late getting back to him. She'd had to do a lot of schedule shuffling to make sure she could make the dead-line, and it had taken some time to set up the interview with Colonel Jackson.

Yet everything seemed to be working out perfectly. Late yesterday afternoon, the colonel had finally returned the call she'd made to his office early Monday morning, explaining that he'd been away on personal business. When she told him what they were planning to do with the story, that they wanted to interview him as part of the broadcast, he said he'd be hon-ored, then graciously offered the use of his office in the Smithsonian Air and Space Museum. By the time they'd hung up, the final arrangements were firmly in place. They would tape the interview a week from today, Wednesday, January 21st, at 10:00 A.M.

Susan had tried to call Neil as soon as she hung up the phone, but no one was home, and his machine hadn't answered. She was anxious to let him know they were going to do the show, that in fact it was already in the works, and she also wanted to invite him to D.C. for the inter-view, as a professional courtesy. Maybe she could spend some time with him afterwards, get more information for the story by talking to him.

She picked up the phone to dial his number. It was only 7:00 A.M. in Pasadena, but she didn't want to risk missing him again. It rang three times before he answered, his voice sounding husky with sleep.

"Thomas residence."

"Neil? Susan Allison. Sorry to call so early, but I'm already late getting back to you."

"Don't worry about it. It's nice to hear your voice again," he said.

"I've got good news. We're going to do your story. I talked to Craig Warren about our meeting Friday, told him what I know of the story so far. He told me to drop everything and do what I had to do to get it aired on Valentine's Day. That's just four weeks from now."

"I don't know what to say," Neil replied, suddenly sounding fully awake. "To tell you the truth, I was beginning to think you'd changed your mind."

"Not at all. In fact, I've already set up an interview with Colonel Jackson. We're going to shoot it at the Smithsonian Air and

Space Museum in Washington, D.C., next Wednesday. I thought you might like to be there for it. It'd give you a chance to see him again, too," Susan offered.

"Actually, I've never met him in person," Neil replied. "We've had several phone conversations, and we've E-mailed each other back and forth, but that's it. I'd love it," he said, then laughed, adding, "I need to use up some frequent flyer miles anyway. I can't think of a better reason."

"Great!" Susan smiled to herself, then went on to give him the details of the interview, including her personal number in case he needed to get in touch with her. She concluded by saying, "So I'll see you Wednesday at ten sharp. I'm looking forward to seeing you again."

She hung up the phone, pleased. She had been completely professional. She would see him again in a week, and she hoped she hadn't given him any reason to suspect that her interest in him and his story was anything other than business.

She would read again tonight, Caroline's Valentine story, and see if she could understand clearly where Neil Thomas was leading her.

The Valentine Story

February 14, 1994
Union Station, Los Angeles, California

Up from the Alameda Street entry, Caroline saw a group of noisy school-children pass by Josiah as he walked away, ignoring their guide's lesson on the history of Union Station. She smiled at the youthful display unfolding before her, resting there with the sound of the playful children echoing in her ears.

As she watched them, her thoughts went back to her days as a schoolteacher. *How I loved the children,* she thought. She had truly been fortunate to have lived her life consumed in caring about the children who had passed through her classroom doors. It all caused her to think back. Each February fourteenth for forty years she had taught her schoolchildren about the lovers' holiday. Gazing up, she pictured herself standing in front of her fourth grade class at Woodland Elementary and recounting her version of the famous Valentine story.

"Class, your attention please. Who can tell me what we are celebrating today?" The entire classroom of children would raise their hands.

"It's Valentine's Day," they would respond in a happy chorus.

"That's right, children. And I want to tell you who Valentine was. There once lived a man who, long ago, died for his beliefs. His name was Saint Valentine. The legend goes that Saint Valentine was a prisoner of an evil king because of his belief in God. He would not deny it," she told her pupils. "Then God sent a miracle," she continued.

"Saint Valentine had a great love for his wife and he wanted to let her know that one last time. He prayed to find a way to tell her. Then a strange thing happened. A pigeon appeared at the prison window. It was one of the pigeons he recognized from his home. He and his children loved to feed the birds and this was a special one that would eat right out of his hand. It brought him comfort to have his little friend there with him and he shared his food every day with the white-and-black spotted creature. He wondered about his problem as he fed the bird.

"There was also a rosebush that grew near the prison window and it had one beautiful red rose on it. He was close enough to touch it and to smell its fragrance. It reminded him of the love he felt for his wife and he wondered how he might get a message to her since he had neither paper nor pen. Then an idea came to him—he could share the rose with his wife! He reached through the bars and gently plucked the rose from the stem. The thorns caused his fingers to bleed, but he didn't care.

"He decided to write words of love on the rose petals and give them to the pigeon. He hoped the bird would take the petals and fly away to his house. He had to hold onto the hope that his wife would find them and know that he loved her.

"He plucked a piece of straw from the pile the guards gave him to sleep on and used the sharp end to press the words, 'I love you' on the petals of the rose. He sent the message, one petal at a time, with the pigeon. The pigeon would take the petal from his hand and quickly fly away. It continued to do the same thing every day until all the petals were gone.

"Then came the appointed day for his execution. Again, the king's emissaries asked him if he would renounce his belief in God. He would not do it. The guards took Saint Valentine and cut off his head. He had been true and faithful: true to his love for his wife, true to his love for his God. *True* love demands a price be paid, an effort made."

The children would always gasp at the part about Saint Valentine's execution; yet she had been determined to instill in them values. Love did not come cheaply. Not true love.

She would continue: "The prison windows had great iron bars to keep the prisoners in, but the bars did not keep Saint Valentine from sending his love out. Saint Valentine was free!"

Invariably the children would furrow their little brows and gaze at her strangely because of the puzzling paradox in her words. Then one brave, inquisitive child would raise his hand and ask, "If there were bars on the windows, and he was in prison, then how was he free?"

"Because when you love," Caroline would answer, "and then when you believe in something as strongly as Saint Valentine did, no one can lock away your love. The jailer can imprison you, but not your feelings. They are always safe, right here," and she would point to the center of her chest.

"No matter what bad things happen to a person, if they feel love for someone and believe in something, then they too are free. The Valentine card is a symbol of love for others and the rose is the symbol of hope and of sharing that love. When you see a rose, think about how Saint Valentine loved his wife and family so very much. And as you grow, look for someone you can love in the same way. And then, every rose will remind you of your special love. It's one reason your daddies may give a rose to your mommies along with a Valentine card."

Again the children would appear a little bewildered, but just as surely, one would also ask, "Did you get a rose from your husband, Mrs. Thomas?"

"Oh yes," she would answer. "Yes! Yes I did, a very long time ago. And I knew he loved me then and I believe he still loves me now."

She wished she had been able to continue teaching but she was getting so forgetful now. Except for daydreaming,

her mind seemed more and more detached.

Caroline fumbled to pick up her
purse from the floor. As she did, her
chest grew tight, her breathing became
labored.

"I forgot to take my pills when I left
this morning—or did I?" she mumbled
in a low voice. She found the prescrip-
tion holder and flipped the long white
top open, her hand trembling. The pills
inside were separated into days. Easy.
So she wouldn't take too many or forget a day. Trouble was, she could
barely remember what day it was. She
would laugh—if the pain wasn't so
great.

Her fingers trembled as she reached
for the small white pills and brought
them to her mouth. She let them sit on
her tongue for a minute, then reached
back down for the small plastic juice
container she'd brought, its plastic
straw already inserted on top. She
coughed as she drank, almost chok-
ing. Struggling, she then relaxed back
in the chair, trying to control her
breathing.

She bent over to return the container to her large black purse. As she did, her hand brushed an envelope. She lifted it out, setting it on her lap with Neil's last letter. Taking deep breaths, she composed herself as best she could, leaning her head on the back of the chair. She glanced at the old clock. 11:00 A.M.

The place was so much the same, but much less busy. Amtrak was the name now. It had been Union Pacific back then. Her mind roamed back as she looked down at the letter.

Neil would need to come for her by 3:00 P.M. That's when the men from the navy said he would be there. That's when they said his remains would be returned to the United States. Neil would keep his promise to her, right here at Union Station. Those were his last words to her. It might've taken fifty years, but she believed in the signs she had seen.

She closed her tired eyes and took deep steady breaths, trying to regain her strength. The pain in her chest seemed to ease. She remembered his first letter as she held on to his last.

Pacific War

March 15, 1944
Pasadena, California

After one long agonizing month, a letter had finally arrived from Neil. Caroline had been fighting her own war, a war of nerves. She anxiously removed the gardening gloves that she wore as she worked the soil around the flower bed. She had seen Mr. Myers, the postman, coming up the street and was hoping he'd turn up the drive to her home.

She had made a point to be out

working in the yard every day for the last week at a quarter to twelve, pretending to busy herself in the yard. She was secretly hoping and praying that she would get her first letter from her husband.

"Hello, Mrs. Thomas. Well, lookie here," Mr. Myers said. "Looks like a letter from someone with the same last name as yours," he teased, holding it up to the sun, as if trying to make out its contents. Her foot tapped impatiently.

"Says U.S. Navy Postal Service, San Francisco. Hmm. Then it must be for you, Mrs. Thomas," he smiled, extending his hand as she reached for the letter.

"Thank you, Mr. Myers," she called as he walked down the driveway. She hurried into the house to sit down and enjoy these first words from her husband. Dropping down on the sofa, she opened the letter.

Somewhere in the Pacific
February 28th, 1944

Dearest Caroline,

I miss you! We shipped out of San Francisco and made it to Pearl Harbor in seven days. The accommodations were spacious—only six pilots to a ten-by-ten bunk room. Because we're replacements, we're awaiting assignments to a carrier. I have a fair idea where we're headed.

The fighting right now is in the Marianas and Caroline Islands. The marines are taking one island at a time, it seems, and the navy is claiming the air and the sea, to cut off the Japs from reinforcing their strongholds.

We certainly can't let them mess with your islands, can we? The Carolines, I mean. It'll bring me good luck to fly out there, you'll see.

I guess you're keeping up on the news down at the theater. If I get on a newsreel, I'll be sure and wave by wagging the wings for you.

How's Johnny and Pete? Have we heard anything? It sounds like it's been

real rough for Johnny over there in It-
aly. That Anzio place is really taking a
beating, from what the Stars and
Stripes *has to say. Hope Pete is out*
here somewhere, giving a hand in that
submarine he got assigned to. I'll feel
a lot better about floating around on a
big flattop, if I know he's working be-
low. We ought to have the Japs licked
soon, coming at 'em both ways.

Pearl Harbor is a sobering sight. The
wreckage from the attack on December
7th, '41 is still visible. It's eerie to think
that the Arizona is now a tomb to a
thousand sailors—makes the war sud-
denly more real to me.

I can't think of a whole lot to say. I
realize it might take awhile to get letters
back and forth. Just write me often. I
live to hear from you.

I made this little paper rose out of
napkins. Maybe I've finally found my
calling, a florist. Well, it's the next best
thing to our garden, and it doesn't need
water.

I pray for you and our baby. I'm
proud to have you for a wife, sweet-

*heart. I love you more than I know how
to say in words.*

Forever is a promise to keep.
Your loving husband,
Neil

*P.S. You won't believe who I saw my
first day in Pearl. Fred Terry, your ex-
fiancé. He says hello. I think losing out
still bugs him. I tried not to rub it in, that
he didn't get to take the prettiest girl
from Eagle Rock to the altar. He's a
typist at the processing center at Naval
H.Q. Tell his folks I saw him and that
he looks great. Why shouldn't he—the
sun and the beach and a cushy job. He
probably got the typing job by being the
fastest to write, "Now is the time for all
good men to come to the aid of their
country." How do some guys rate?*

Caroline carefully folded and placed
the two-page letter back into its envelope and put it in the end table drawer.
She had been sending letters through
the naval post office with his name,
rank, and serial number, and she

hoped they were getting to him. He sounded good, and hearing from him had soothed her frazzled nerves.

She was dealing remarkably well, she thought, with their separation. It was good to stay busy every afternoon at the Jensen Theater. Working at the ticket booth gave her the opportunity to see a lot of old friends and exchange news on how things were going for all the boys.

Weeks passed before she heard from him again. She was out in the yard, hoping as usual that the postman would bring her the letter she longed for. He always had some new quip about who was sending the letters from the Pacific. She had gotten used to knowing by the look on his face if he was carrying a letter from Neil.

"How're the flowers, Caroline?" Mr. Myers asked soberly, startling her. She was down on her hands and knees, working a new area of soil in the garden.

"Oh!" she said, throwing her hand to

her chest as she turned, getting up. "How'd you sneak up on me?" She brushed off the full one-piece dress, now far along in her pregnancy, and removed her gardening gloves.

"Practice," he replied, his voice serious as he gave her the mail in his hand.

"You don't seem your normal self, Mr. Myers. Is something wrong?" Caroline's brow creased with worry as she reached for the mail. She quickly looked through, making sure there wasn't a telegram.

"I've had to deliver two Western Unions today. It's almost more than I can take sometimes. I know all these people, their boys. I don't know why they all seem to hit at once, but they do. This time, one of the boys was Ricky Bell. Killed over Germany in a bomber. He was a gunner. That boy was really something. And only eighteen years old, too."

Caroline gasped at the news. He told her that the other was Bob "Lightning" Richards, a star football player from high school and good friend of Neil's.

He was married and had one child, a daughter. She hurt for the families. She felt sorry for them, but relief for herself. Her eyes filled with tears.

"I'm sorry if I upset you, sweetheart. I didn't mean to," Mr. Myers went on, the dull expression on his face telling Caroline how much he hated the deadly business that was taking their best men away from them. "Looks like a letter from someone in there that you should probably go read. It'll make you feel better. Have a nice day, young lady. Don't worry." He turned slowly to walk away.

Caroline liked him. He was clearly a sensitive man and there weren't enough of those in the world. "Thank you, Mr. Myers," she called. He waved in acknowledgment.

Tossing her gardening gloves on the porch swing, she opened the door and went into the house, kicking off her shoes in the entry. She curled up on the sofa, then opened the letter.

July 6, 1944
USS Princeton, *South Pacific*

Dearest Caroline,

You must know from the newsreels what's happening out here. We've been chasing Japs from island to island.

I guess you ought to know some other things, too. I've been holding a lot inside. Every time I think I've just about got the worst battle experiences behind me, something new happens that humbles me. Flight training is one thing—I won't kid you, sweetheart. But dodging bullets is a totally different story. I wondered if I should talk about it to you, or if I should just gloss over the fact that this business out here is a far different life-and-death struggle than one imagines, even if you're watching actual film footage from the front lines.

War isn't the glory thing Hollywood makes it up to be. It hurts a lot of people. When one of your friends gets it, there's no band playing, no bugler playing taps, no marches in parades, no speeches, no one waving a flag—

nothing that can make up for the loss when your buddy takes a hit and goes down, then disappears under the waves of the Pacific.

Listen, honey. This thing is for keeps for a lot of guys. I just don't want you to feel like I'm alone, or that you are. There are a lot of married guys out here, and a million men at war in the Pacific. The odds are on our side that I can come out of this okay. Please know that I'm doing my best. But if something happens, it's no less fair than what's happened to other guys.

I know you don't want to hear this, but I want at least one of my letters to be as honest as possible so that you know I believe. What I'm trying to say is that I believe there's a God who knows us and our situations, and if my time is up—well, I believe He'll make everything right for you and me. I'm not going to do anything stupid, but I've got to tell you that it's angered me more than once to have Japs shooting back at me.

The good news is that I've definitely been protected plenty, and I attribute that to your prayers. I feel them, and I'm encouraged by that. Keep it up. We'll have this thing over with soon.

Things are heating up. The pressure is really on the Japs. We're leapfrogging from one island to the next. Within a year, we'll be knocking on Tokyo's door.

I guess I'm telling you this because I want to get it off my chest. I also want you to know that I believe we're engaged in a just cause here. I couldn't do this if I thought for one minute that we're not.

From the time I saw the Arizona *sitting on the bottom of Pearl Harbor, with a thousand soldiers buried inside, I've known that we're fighting for peace. Ironic, isn't it? Just be proud of us and pray for us. I'll be more cheerful now.*

How's our boy? I guess I think the baby's going to be a boy. Got the picture two days ago of you in front of the garden. You've really been working hard. It looks great! How come you're so beautiful, no matter how big you get?

How I wish I could be there with you. I want you to know that I'm praying for you. I want you to be at peace. I'll come home to you. Don't worry, sweetheart. I'll keep my promise, and we'll plant flowers together, and go to Rose Parades together for fifty more years. You'll see. You are my inspiration, and I need you.

I've got to close for now. You're the first thing on my mind when I wake up, and the last thing I think about when I hit the sack at night.

Caroline, don't let all the stuff I've said in this letter get you down. Even roses have thorns. I love you with all my heart. Take good care of our kid! Forever—a promise to keep!

Your loving husband,
Neil

The letter disturbed her, fanning her deepest anxieties; but she understood that he had to try to tell her about his fear, or she might not understand if something happened to him. She had never heard him talk so openly about the danger.

The words, "Even roses have thorns." She knew what he meant. She knew he was tough. He had to be. It must really be getting to him, or he wouldn't have been so brutally honest.

She continued to follow every bit of news from the Pacific Theater. The enemy was tenacious. War. Thorns indeed. *Is he being shot at today?* she wondered. *Is he shooting at someone else, strafing an enemy ship with a hundred guns pointed at him?* It was all too much to think about. She had to know, but at the same time she had shut it out of her mind.

Once the thorns were removed, they would celebrate their love together, and never be separated again.

October 14, 1944
U.S. Fifth Fleet, Task Force 58
Aircraft Carrier USS Princeton

Lieutenant Thomas was taking his dinner at a relaxed pace while he read the *Stars and Stripes.* Things were swinging the Allies' way on all fronts. He reflected on the ten months of war he had experienced. He considered how he had built up a shell to keep him from thinking about the killing and the loss of friends. He wondered about his surviving brother, Johnny, over in Italy, and what he must be going through.

In ten months, he had experienced more danger, more fear, more loss of friends, and more of a part in killing than a hundred men his age would ever experience outside the elements of battle and war.

He considered the killing capability of modern weapons, something the world had never experienced before. The slaughter of millions had taken place in World War I, "the war to end all wars," and it had been brutal. But the awesomeness of destruction that could be wrought on an enemy force by a single well-armed plane was almost incomprehensible.

This war was hundreds of times more deadly from above than anything ever imagined before. One good hit with a well-placed five-hundred-pound bomb or torpedo could cost the enemy hundreds, even thousands of lives in a matter of seconds. With hundreds of planes moving in at one another at speeds up to four hundred miles per hour, Neil and his comrades in their F6F Hellcat fighters were frightening in the extent of damage they could inflict. The pilot seat wasn't only a seat in a deadly piece of machinery, but a witness seat in a court of war that was rapidly heading toward higher levels of mechanized destruction.

Caroline. How was she doing? he wondered. What was she doing? Their little boy had come a month early. How he wanted to be there. Home. The sweetest place on earth.

The war. It was a just cause. It was for them, his wife and his kid. If it wasn't for that, he could never do it. It had to be just.

"Hey, Neil, ol' buddy. What ya say I join ya." Lt. Comdr. Chad Watson sat down at the mess table with his tray opposite Neil. "How's the war going for our comrades in Europe?" he asked.

Neil looked up from his paper and smiled, "The Nazis are getting their fannies kicked, Skipper. I've got a brother on the ground somewhere over there." He smiled as if suggesting Johnny's boots were doing the kicking. "If anybody can kick hard, it's my older brother." He laughed.

Commander Watson smiled, seeing the affectionate look on his lieutenant's face. "I guess I owe you congratulations. Some of the boys told me your wife gave birth to a son. I'm real happy for you, Neil."

"Oh, yeah, I almost forgot." Neil reached inside his shirt pocket and pulled out a cigar. "I saved this for you." He handed the red-and-white-banded cigar over the table to the squadron commander.

"Thanks." Watson held it to his nose and asked, "Cuban?"

"The best," said Thomas. "Bought 'em in LA the day I shipped out. Thought it'd be good to have them to celebrate with when the big day came. Funny. I don't even smoke."

"A good smoke now and then would do you good, Neil," replied Watson, grinning as he slipped the cigar in his pocket, then started to eat.

There was a pause while they worked at their food. Neil was just about done, getting ready to head back to his quarters, when his commander spoke up.

"You've got seven kills, Thomas. Today could've been your eighth. What's wrong, Neil?" he queried his wing leader. The seriousness in his lieutenant smelled like stress, like fear. He had seen it before. It could get a man killed if he didn't get a grip on it.

"I froze," Neil shot back, looking up at the commander with apparent ambivalence. "I don't know why. I just froze. I'm sorry."

"Is it your boy, being a new dad?"

"No, sir."

"Look, sometimes it happens. We start thinking about the wife and kids and we get cautious, tense, lose the aggressive edge. But losing that edge has gotten a lot of good pilots killed."

The commander looked at Neil as he continued to eat. "I'm giving you some leave time," he ordered, his mouth full of food. "Unwind. We need you, Thomas. We don't need you dead. No missions for a few days. I want you on the bridge. Work with Captain Keller. I've already talked to him about it. It will give you some good experience, besides."

"Listen, sir. I appreciate what you're trying to do, but—"

Watson cut him off. "I don't need more dead pilots, damn it!" he responded, jabbing his fork toward Thomas's face. "You deserve the break. I'm not picking on you, Thomas. It happens to the best of us. And, frankly, you're one of them. I'm the commander here, and it's my squadron. If we get into trouble, then the leave is off. But for now, no missions for a week."

He glared at Neil sternly and shoveled another fork of potatoes into his mouth. "Oh, yeah. I almost forgot," he went on. "Once this next campaign is over, I'll be sending you and Bobby down to Australia. We've got some new F6Fs to pick up. Take some time. Have some fun. Know what I mean?" The commander winked.

"Oh, and Thomas," Watson looked up from his food, "the brass says we'll be opening the way for the Army Air Corps in the Philippines. It all starts in a couple of days. It shouldn't take too long before the army has a couple of airstrips. Then we'll turn it over to them. Get some rest." He turned back to concentrate on his plate.

"Thank you, sir. Is that all?" Neil stood up to leave.

"That's all, Thomas. Loosen up, boy."

Neil saluted and left. Dropping his tray off, he headed out of the officers' mess, down the stairs to the pilots' quarters and the bunk room he shared with Ens. Bobby Roberts.

He was uptight and he knew it. He hated what he was becoming. *Yeah, sure,* he reasoned silently, *it was a duty, war, that's all. Them or me.* Talking to himself, trying to get geared up for battle. He was slipping. It was more than the battle taking place in the Pacific skies. It was the war going on inside him that worried him most. Had he gotten soft? Was he afraid of something, something bigger than dying?

What would he be when he came

home? How would he act? Would he be a psychopathic, hate-filled killer, or just an ex–U.S. Navy pilot? A hero who did his job well, killed well? He wasn't sure what was eating at him, but it was eating him from the inside out.

Neil thought about the Nip that Watson had splashed that day. He replayed the whole scene in a matter of seconds on his way to his bunk room. It should have been his kill, an easy kill. It would have been his eighth. He had the Jap on the run. Like a movie, he could see the fight, could see the Jap Zero in his gunsights.

He not only froze with the Jap in his sights and his finger on the trigger of the six wing-mounted, .50-cal. machine guns—he had some crazy thought go through his head when he should have been concentrating on combat. It had never happened before.

There was the enemy fighter, a Zero, the sole survivor of a group of six fighters that Neil and his squadron had just tangled with. His thumb was on the trigger. He watched the Jap pilot maneuvering wildly, trying to escape. But Neil had him cold. The Jap would die in seconds when he let go with a burst from the machine guns.

Then something happened. He couldn't do it. The callous shell of protection a pilot must throw up around himself had broken.

An image had flashed through his mind like a scene in a movie. It was Cameron. He could see Jim Cameron running, two Jap Zeros on his tail. It had happened one month earlier, over the island of Tinian. He and Jimmy, accompanied by a new guy, Ensign Roberts, were caught off guard. Jimmy decided to try a maneuver to draw off one of the Jap fighters, but two followed him instead. Neil and the new guy, tangled up with two other Jap planes, got lucky and splashed the Zeros, then went to help out Jimmy, who was frantically calling for backup. He could still hear Jim's voice over the radio.

"I can't shake these guys! Where are you, Neil? Oh, man, I'm hit. I'm going down! May Day! May Day! Anybody read me? Come on, Thomas—you there?"

Neil called back, "We're on our way, Jimmy. Hold on, buddy. Go down if you're hit. Maybe they'll peel off of you and we can pick 'em up. Jimmy?" He heard no response.

He caught sight of the aerial duel— what was left of it. They had Jimmy, and he was going down on the deck, flying just above the surface of the water, followed by the Zeros. He was smoking, fire coming out of his fuselage. But the Tojos showed no mercy, no mercy at all. They fired at him again, making sure he wouldn't survive. Jimmy's plane broke apart from the impact of hitting the water.

Neil had been filled with white-hot rage. A feeling of hate swept over him. He closed in from twelve o'clock, coming in on them out of the sun, with Bobby Roberts right behind. He opened up immediately, nailing one Jap pilot cold. He saw him get hit as the .50-cal. bullets tore the canopy to shreds, then watched as bits and pieces of airplane exploded around him. He felt satisfied that he'd evened the score. He watched what was left of the Nip's plane cartwheel and skip across the waves—kill number seven.

Bobby was chasing the other one. After a minute of dueling, he had made his second kill.

Neil turned back and flew over the spot where Jimmy Cameron had gone down, hoping beyond hope that Jimmy had somehow gotten out of the cockpit, was down there alive. But no sign. His buddy had been swallowed up in the great expanse of ocean, as if nothing had taken place.

It was strange. His fellow pilot and comrade flying next to him one minute, then gone the next. Not a trace that he had even existed. Nothing to say. Nothing to do. Just fly back to the carrier.

Neil entered the deck hallway to his quarters, his mind far from that day when they'd lost Jimmy Cameron. His thoughts had shifted to the scene of the dogfight on that morning's mission. He could see himself, the enemy plane in his sights. He could see the moment when he should have blasted the Jap out of the sky, but he'd frozen instead.

With his thumb on the trigger he could down the Nip. More payback. But the thoughts of the two Jap pilots who hadn't shown mercy to Jimmy one month earlier had a sudden and un-expected effect on him. In his mind, he saw Jimmy instead of the enemy pilot, trying desperately to live, to survive, to get back home to his wife and little girl.

He had hesitated as that image had flashed before him, and he couldn't kill the Jap. If he did, it'd be just the same as killing the man's wife, child, his mother or father.

His bravado vanished. He lost his edge. His inaction could cost another American his life, and he knew it. Then the skipper moved in. Watson yelled over the radio for him to get out of the way or get shot down, then moved in and splashed the Jap. It was over. The ocean took the Jap and his fighter and swallowed them, just like it had with Jimmy.

Neil opened the metal door to his cabin and entered the small cubicle. He was confused. He was supposed to be a killer. It's what he was paid to do. It was war.

He sat on the edge of his bunk, staring at the floor, knowing that Watson was right. He needed a break, to sort the strange feeling out. If he didn't, it might cost him his life next time.

He swung his legs onto the bed and lay back, hands behind his head, looking up at the ceiling. He saw Caroline and the rose garden on Marengo Avenue. He pictured his little boy playing there. He was suddenly sick of the violence, afraid of the prospects of growing stone cold, insensitive, mean.

Reaching over for the picture of his wife he had pinned to the wall, he brought it down and laid it on his chest, his thoughts still uneasy. He had become a killer. He had lost everything gentle since the last time he'd touched her. But the people back home would call him an "ace," patting him on the back when he returned home. Five kills plus two. He was good at it.

He tried to put aside the self-pity, the remorse over the Japs he had killed. But it wasn't remorse. They were trying to kill him and were just as dedicated to their job as he was to his. It was a fair duel when he tangled with an enemy pilot. The best, or luckiest, won. Nothing more. Killing happened. But he was afraid he would never be the same, feel the same about life—about love.

He had to fight this new battle with an unfamiliar inner voice. He had to get back to the love that used to sing in his heart, the carefree spirit that made life so meaningful. Caroline, their new little house, simple dreams, peace.

He wanted the war to be over. He wanted to go home. He had a promise to keep by their anniversary, February 14th.

After these many months the wind of war was blowing west, to the Philippines. Perhaps they could get this thing over with soon, and all the foreboding, the mixed-up emotions, could be left out in the Pacific where they belonged. Buried at sea.

War. It could kill men's souls as well. He suddenly thought about that day on Santa Monica Beach back in February, a few days before he'd shipped out. He and Caroline had gone there to be near the ocean and walk along the beach at sunset. He'd picked up a seashell and handed it to her. Lying on his bunk with his hands behind his head, he could see himself with Caroline.

"Here. Listen, Neil," she said, handing the shell back to him. "What do you hear, honey?"

"The sounds of peace," was his quiet reply.

"Don't you hear the ocean, the waves?" she teased, poking him in the ribs.

His mind was on a visit he'd made to see Father O'Donnell. He looked down at her with a weak grin and simply said, "Peace."

What had Father O'Donnell told him? What was it? Neil had gone to St. Andrew's looking for a benediction of sorts, not a lecture.

"Keep your head and your heart linked together, Neil. Don't fear the death of the body, boy." Father O'Donnell always called him that. "Boy." "Fear the death of love. No one can take that from you, Neil. No one. Only you can let it die, and you can't let it die. Fear hate and anger as if they were cancer. Take care, my boy. Here's a Scripture from Proverbs I want you to reflect on. Read them out loud."

Keep thy heart with all diligence,
for out of it are the issues of life.

"No matter what happens, don't let any man take your heart," the priest continued. "Know what's most important, then do it. As you do, your life will be well spent. There's nothing more tragic than one who lives a life filled with petty and unimportant things. To know what matters most, you've got to keep your heart."

It was the last visit he'd had with his friend, the good father. He had shared other thoughts with him, reminding him of his good family and the catechisms. Then he prayed with him and gave him final confession before Neil headed for combat.

But those words. Words about love, the heart, what matters most. The words seemed like idle banterings of a pious man who didn't understand how much Neil cared about the life of his body. He thought the old priest was just trying to do his duty. Yet Father O'Donnell was an ex–U.S. Army chaplain. He had seen men die in World War I. Maybe the priest had seen something or knew something that Neil could only know after tasting the bitterness of battle. Now he knew that the old priest had been wise.

He felt the warmth of love through distant recall of memories. Could that die? Could the ability to love be hardened or lost because of the killing he was experiencing? He pondered long and hard on the questions.

He couldn't fathom love dying—then. He felt so full of it—then. Before he had killed, before he had tasted war's ugliness, before he had become an "ace."

Neil pondered Father O'Donnell's words as he stared at the photograph. Love. Peace. War. One preceded the other. Which one, though?

He thought back to that day on the beach. He remembered Caroline's questioning look when he'd said the word "peace." His mind had been on what was out there, out there in the Pacific, six thousand miles beyond Santa Monica Pier.

"What does Pacific mean in Spanish, Caroline?" he recalled asking. He thought it meant calm or something.

"Pacifico," she said, "means 'peaceful,' 'tranquil.'" She had looked up at him with a confused look, wondering what he was thinking.

Pacific. Pacific war. He turned to her. "Peaceful war," he joked in a quiet tone, indicating the irony of it. They had walked down the beach until it grew dark. His eyes were on the west, the setting sun. It was a rising sun for others. Soon he would be with them.

Raven Leader

October 20, 1944
Gulf of Leyte off the Philippine coast

Lieutenant Thomas put down his pen and read the letter he had been writing. It was man talk. How do you tell a woman about war, the way it really is, without depressing the hell out of her? The one thing he wanted most? To share what he was going through; not just the military stuff, but what he was feeling on the inside and what was causing it from the outside. But then— everything he felt on the inside had to do with outside events. Aircraft cours-ing through the air at speeds of up to four hundred miles per hour. So much enemy fire coming at you. It was all in the hands of God. All of it.

God. He knew God was real now. Not because of war, but in spite of it. There must be a devil, too, he mused. Evil, hate, death, war. It all contrasted so diametrically with goodness, love, life, peace. The only person he could talk to was God. Or Caroline.

He looked down at the letter again. He read the writing, his attempt to get it all out. He knew if women could see this first-hand, war would probably end.

They'd ban it! They'd hold out their most precious feminine offering from men until they all surrendered and signed peace treaties with one another. He smiled at the weird thoughts. Strange thoughts, but probably accu-rate. For him, now, women and sanity seemed to go hand in hand. They had the sensitivity and instincts to find a better way. The ability to perceive the insanity of it all.

"It's a big operation, Caroline." He

frowned, crumpled the letter up, threw it in the wastebasket, and walked out of the briefing room. The censors would probably cut it all up anyway.

Lieutenant Thomas had an uneasy feeling. The attack against targets in Manila would commence at 0600 hours. The planes were on deck even as he filed out of the briefing room with Bobby Roberts and a new pilot by the name of Tony Martinez. Tony was from Oxnard, California, just up the road from LA. Neil liked him and vowed to take extra care of the new guy.

He didn't like it when that uneasy feeling came over him. It usually meant someone was going to die—one of his men or someone in the squadron. He knew the possibility existed that it could be himself. He just had to suck it in and do his job. Everyone depended on him being there for them.

It was big. This operation was backed by an armada of over a thousand warships. The Seventh Fleet, under Admiral Kincaid, and the Third Fleet, under Adm. W. F. "Bull" Halsey, were out to crush the naval and land forces of Imperial Japan in preparation for the move against mainland Japan itself. The first order of business was the "back door." The Allies could not afford to allow the Japanese to have over 300,000 men behind them as they approached the islands near Japan. They must wipe out the enemy's ability to reinforce troops from the Philippines.

The big day the Filipinos had been waiting for was coming soon. MacArthur, commander of Allied forces in the Pacific, had promised he would return. After three long and bloody years of war, today he would do so.

The planes were on the flight deck. Pilots were headed toward their F6F Hellcat fighters. Each plane carried ammo for the six .50-cal. machine guns and two 500-lb. bombs. Their primary mission was bomber protection and strafing of enemy targets, but today they were to be prepared to take on any enemy ship or target that could threaten the invasion—poised to lead the liberation of the Philippines from the air.

THE LAST VALENTINE   131

"So it's Manila and Clark Field," Lt. J. G. Billings commented to Neil.

"Yeah. You look out for yourself, Billings. By the way, congratulations on your promotion. The guys in Raven 2 are some of the best. You'll do fine as their leader." He could tell how nervous the young twenty-one-year-old lieutenant was. He felt the same way, but hoped he didn't show it.

Billings gave him the thumbs-up sign and split off to his flight division, which was positioned ahead of Neil's group.

Neil's division was known by the call sign Raven 3. All of its flyers were under twenty-five years of age. At twenty-six, he was the old man. "How you feeling today, Tony?" asked a confident-acting, smiling Lieutenant Thomas to the new guy, as he patted him on the back.

"A little nervous, Skipper," came the reply.

"You just follow Bobby and me. Remember what you've learned and you'll be okay."

"Aye, aye, Lieutenant," said the anxious young pilot, with a look on his face that said, "If you say so."

"Every new pilot goes through the same thing. Just ask Bobby here. He splashed two Zeros in his first week. No sweat. Right, Roberts?" Everyone seemed to look to the lieutenant for assurance and support.

Bobby, staring off toward the planes taking off, was busily engaged in his chewing gum. They would get their call any second to man the planes. "Yeah, that's right, Skipper. No sweat," he replied.

"Okay, gentlemen. Our turn. Let's go." Lieutenant Thomas called out above the cacophony as they were given the signal to board their Hellcats.

Every new pilot goes through the jitters, he was thinking as he ran to his plane. *Man, I go through this every time I take off. Every combat mission makes my hands sweat.* The uneasy feeling he was trying to put aside was still with him. The older pilots had the same fears and anxieties as the newer ones, they just learned how to swagger through. Becoming cavalier about facing death was a way of coping.

He pulled himself up into the cockpit. The wind was high and the noise from the engines was deafening.

"Hey, Lieutenant," came a shout from the deck. It was Johnson, the crew chief.

"Yeah, what is it?" The petty officer had something in his hands.

"You dropped something," he called over the noise, holding it up for the lieutenant to see.

"Oh, yeah. Thanks." Neil motioned for Johnson to climb up on the wing.

Johnson handed the lieutenant a small brown paper package. "Good hunting, Skipper!" he shouted over the din. Then he jumped back down to the deck. He gave him a salute, which was returned by Neil's grin and a thumbs-up.

Lieutenant Thomas, his hand to his throat-collar mike, was now giving the flight command to his pilots. They began to taxi out.

He reached into his Mae West's zipper pocket, took the small brown package out and kissed it. Replacing it, he zipped the pocket securely and offered a silent prayer followed by the sign of the cross, his way of settling into the mission. Once he had done that, he focused. The small package contained a framed picture of Caroline and three-month-old Neil Junior. He didn't have time to read the letter. Mail call was just minutes after the briefing; now he had something to look forward to after this morning's mission. Wrapped up in the brown package, Neil had placed his "good luck" charm, the Valentine with the crushed red rose given to him by Caroline at Union Station. It had always brought him back safe, and he promised to return it to her—safe.

He taxied into position. That gnawing, uneasy feeling—he fought it through his mechanical flight check as he waited for the signal to take off. The flag dropped. He gave his engine full throttle. In minutes he was airborne, his squadron alongside him.

"Okay, gentlemen, listen up. We will be on radio silence after this. Our objective is Red Bird. I repeat, Red Bird.

Everybody got that?" They all acknowledged with a "Roger, Skipper." Red
Bird was the code name for strafing
Clark Airfield, the U.S. Army air base
that had fallen with the Philippines to
the Japanese. Planes from the *Princeton* were attacking with two objectives:
One, Clark Field, the other, Manila itself.

Within thirty minutes they sighted the
billowing smoke from the other squadron's attack on Manila fuel depots and
shipping. They were headed north-
west, over the Sierra Madre mountain
range and into the center of Luzon itself. No enemy aircraft had been
sighted. They had caught the Japs flat-
footed.

"Okay, boys. There's our target.
Eleven o'clock. Let's knock 'em out
with one big punch—then we go home.
Follow me in." Lieutenant Thomas
banked hard to the left and each of the
Hellcats followed.

"Stay close in, Tony, and just follow
Bobby."

"Aye, aye, Skipper," the new pilot
said.

They made two passes through heavy antiaircraft fire. One of the planes was hit instantly, Wilkerson's.

"Looks like I caught some fire, L.T.," Wilkerson radioed. "My right wing flap. I've lost a little oil pressure, too."

"Okay, Wilk. Let's see if you can nurse your baby home."

"Roger, Skipper."

Their first mission of the invasion over the Philippines went better than he had expected. One plane hit, but no losses. Not yet, at least. Lieutenant Thomas looked over to his right wing man. There was Tony Martinez with a thumbs-up.

"Looks like we left 'em smokin', huh, Lieutenant?" The voice was Martinez's.

"We sure did. A fine job, Tony. You get a couple of Zeros there on the ground?"

"Yes, sir. Only three to go until I'm an ace, right?" the young pilot joked.

"Sorry, Martinez. They have to be airborne—at least one foot off the ground. That's the rules of the game." It was Ensign Roberts.

"Yeah, them's the rules, Martinez,"

chimed in Wilkerson, as he guided his smoking Hellcat back toward the carrier. It helped calm him to be part of the ongoing chatter.

"Raven leader to Raven 3. Raven leader to Raven 3, come in, Raven 3." It was the squadron commander, Chad Watson.

"This is Raven 3. I read you, Raven leader. Go ahead," Neil radioed back.

"Raven 3. What kind of shape you in?"

"All accounted for, sir. Wilkerson hit, nursing it, and we're headed home."

"I've got a little change in plans. We need you to make a run against Black Dog. Come in."

"Aye, aye, Skipper. Same coordinates per game plan?"

"Same, Raven 3. Send Wilkerson home. We'll keep radio contact with him."

"Roger, Raven leader." Neil hated abandoning any of his men. But they all knew the score. The mission came first.

"Okay. Listen up, gentlemen. Raven leader gave us a little follow-up mission. The target is Black Dog. I repeat, the target is Black Dog. Wilk, I hate to do this, but you're on your own. Maintain radio contact with Raven leader at," and he gave Wilkerson the radio frequency. "We'll follow your flight path back home. You read me?"

"Roger. I copy that, L.T." Ensign Wilkerson saluted as the group peeled off to head south for Manila.

Within seconds they had Manila's docks in sight. The previous bombing runs had awakened the sleeping enemy and they had opened up with a fury from every gun emplacement not destroyed by the previous waves of American planes.

"Okay, boys, one run and we're home free. Let's make it a good one. Follow me in." Lieutenant Thomas peeled off to a hard two o'clock and headed into the firing, which was creating puffs of black smoke around his cockpit. He was headed for the ships that were still afloat and returning fire at the American planes. "Remember Pearl Harbor!" he voiced as he let go with every gun he had. He pulled up hard, felt a thud as his plane shook around him. He had been hit, but the plane was still manageable.

He glanced back at the ship he had just strafed. A ball of flames shot up into the air. "Bingo!" he exclaimed, as the explosion was followed by a second and then a third.

They regrouped at 10,000 feet. A plane was missing.

"Where's Martinez?" Thomas called over the radio to Ensign Roberts.

"He was right behind me. Perry, did you see Martinez?"

Perry had just joined them. "Yeah. He got it. Saw him get hit and then he took it into the docks. No chance of getting out."

"Damn!" Instantly Lieutenant Thomas was filled with the same rage he felt over the downing of Jimmy Cameron months before. Rage and violence go hand in hand. It was the only way he could make sense of the killing and destruction. He was glad he felt it. It allowed him to cope with the lunacy of it all, the confusion that kept playing its bitter melody inside his head.

"Hey, Skipper, you don't look so good yourself. You got oil starting to make a mess of things. You got a good chunk of fuselage gone, too."

"Yeah, I know." Neil had to get control of himself. They were over Manila Bay, heading west. He had only two options, really. He could try to make it back to the *Princeton,* one hundred miles offshore to the east of Luzon, or he could ditch in the bay. If he tried to make it back and had to bail out over Luzon, he would face capture from an enemy that beheaded their prisoners. If he ditched it in the bay, there was a chance he'd be picked up by a sub or rescue plane. He felt safer with the latter option.

"Looks like I'm a swimmer today, Bobby. You're Raven 3 now." Just then his plane stuttered. He felt a jolt. Oil engulfed the canopy. "This baby just froze up on me. Can't see a thing. I'm going down. Get me some help, fast. You copy, Bobby?" Lieutenant Thomas opened his canopy for visual help in piloting the Hellcat down toward the sea.

He looked over at his wingman, Roberts.

"Roger that, Skipper," the ensign said. "We're calling for the cavalry now, sir. You hang in there. If you can't, nobody can."

"Thanks, Bobby. Follow me down and then get back home." Neil struggled to level out his plane at five hundred feet. He didn't like the idea of jumping out of a perfectly good airplane, as he had joked to his paratrooper brother two years earlier.

"Bobby?"

"Yeah, Skipper?"

"There are only two things that fall out of the sky. You know what they are?"

Roberts laughed nervously. "Yeah, Skipper. I think I do. Fools and bird—"

"That's right. I want to make sure no one thinks of me as either." Thomas angled his plane into the surf below. Pulling hard on the stick, and with the engine freezing up, he was in a glider against the wind.

"Just a wet deck on a bobbing carrier," he reassured his fellow pilots. His tail hit the water first, dragging the plane to a skipping halt. The nose hit a small wave, causing him to strike his head hard against the instrument panel. He was bleeding, but alive.

"Roberts to Thomas," came the anxious voice over the radio.

"I'm okay, Bobby. It's a rough ride down here. Breaking out the raft."

Ensign Roberts looked on as his comrade climbed up and out of the cockpit and onto the wing of his plane, which was barely afloat. He saw the life raft inflate as he radioed a May Day distress call for his flight leader. His signal was received; he gave the ship the coordinates for the downed pilot.

"Good luck, Skipper," Bobby said to himself. "Okay, boys, we're going home." He swooped low over his friend Thomas, wagging his wings to let him know he had called in the May Day. With a deep feeling of resignation, Bobby offered a silent prayer for his lieutenant.

For two nights in a row he had been with her in her dreams, wearing his uniform. Neil was happy, he was home; but it seemed somehow strange.

Yet the dream gave her a warm feeling, as warm as his touch always gave her. He was holding her in his arms. They were standing among the roses. He brushed the back of his hand gently against her cheeks as she stood there, her eyes closed, feeling his tenderness. He spoke.

"I came to tell you I love you, Caroline." He looked at her with an intensity that seemed to ask silently, Do you understand? He held her hands to his chest, cupping them in his.

"I've never loved you more, and I finally know the word for all of my feelings for you. I know the word"—then he would turn to the rose bush and pick a long-stemmed single red rose in full blossom.

"Your hands are bleeding, Neil. The thorns—they're hurting you. Let me go and get some bandages," she would say to him in the dream.

"No! Don't leave. Not yet. It doesn't hurt anymore. Nothing hurts anymore.

Caroline, the thorns don't hurt. The thorns are a very important part of life."

Why? she could remember thinking, and it was as if he could read her mind.

"Because love means more, grows deeper, if you can overcome the thorns." He then kissed her softly and tenderly.

Looking at her, as he slowly pulled away, he would say, "The thorns attack everyone. Can you do it, Caroline?" and he appeared to have an anxious expression on his face, a pleading look.

She melted into his arms for one final embrace. Then she was left standing there, watching him disappear into a bank of fog. He would turn, in the dream, and would think the question so clearly that she would know he was asking, "Can you do it?" "Do what?" she would question back but he would be gone.

She wanted to run to him but her legs were heavy, as heavy as lead. They wouldn't move.

"I'll be back for you," he seemed to call from the fog-enshrouded field.

Somehow she felt right, even though she couldn't run to him. She felt a peace and a warmth, the way she'd always felt when he was there with her. She accepted it, but not without tears. She would awaken with moist eyes. But she knew he had to leave, as if it were a duty. Just as if one more mission needed to be flown before he could finally return home to her.

Caroline was grateful to wake and feel as if he had been with her in the night. She found herself praying for the dreams to return.

Then the swallow had invaded her peace: *La golondrina.* It appeared at her window on the morning of the second dream-filled night. She suspected the truth would lie in what the postman would be delivering to her that day.

I've got to get out of this bird, Neil thought. He scrambled up and out of the cockpit onto the wing of his Hellcat, now bouncing on the waves. He inflated his life raft, waved a hand signal to Ensign Roberts, who was wagging his fighter's wings in a signal.

Easing into the rubber raft, Neil tried to paddle away, but the waves kept pushing him back toward the plane, which was slowly starting to sink.

"God, let me live," he mumbled aloud. He felt dizzy. The whack on the head must have been harder than he had thought. Blood streamed down his face from a cut over his right eye. He pulled a handkerchief out of his trouser pockets and held it to the wound.

"Let me get out of this to see my wife and kid. God, if you can hear me, I—" Neil blacked out and fell prostrate in the small raft.

He drifted for hours, fading in and out of consciousness. Every now and then a swell would lift his body up, then send him and the raft down the other side. It started to rain. He wondered where the rescue planes were. He hoped for a submarine, seaplane, someone to see him. He knew the navy would be looking for him. He remembered one case where Admiral Spruance held up his entire task force for two hours while they searched for one downed pilot. The memory gave him hope. The waves and the rain were getting stronger. He had to just hold on, just a little while longer. "Got to keep myself alert, watch for the plane," he whispered under his breath. The storm grew more violent. It took everything he had to hold on.

Hours passed. As did, at last, the storm. When night fell the moon reflected an eerie light that shimmered across a vast expanse of water. He was in Manila Bay, floating—floating among sharks, Jap patrol boats, but, hopefully too, a friendly sub.

He longed to be home. Home in Caroline's arms. Home with his little boy. Pasadena, California, had the sweetest ring in the world to it, he thought. What he wouldn't give to be there with his wife and kid. But he couldn't think of that now, could he?

Neil's mind was wandering. It was wandering in an effort to stay alert, alive. His body was drained from its efforts to stay afloat, bail out water, paddle, keep awake.

He hadn't had real sleep for over thirty-six hours. He was glad for one thing, though. He was glad that the sea had become a calm surface. With the moon out now, he could see the silhouette of a mountain range above the distant shoreline. He estimated it to be only five miles away. With any luck, and help from the current and his paddling, he might make it to shore before sunrise.

He began to talk to himself. "I've got to live! For Caroline. Okay. Think, Neil— You've got a kid now. For little Neil. Come on, man, you can do it." He put his effort into paddling and continued to talk to himself. He kept his thoughts focused on home, on Caroline and the baby. Belief, the substance of things hoped for. He envisioned his home and the message on the sign nailed over the front door.

Come on, Neil—they're waiting on the shore. Come on, man, just make it to shore. You can do it! His thoughts weren't the only source of his strength. He believed in God and the help he might get from his weak prayers, but he also needed these images of the stately house on Marengo Avenue—

the same images he used every time he took off for another combat mission.

He visualized holding Caroline there in the rose garden. He visualized handing her a rose. And he visualized asking her to be tough for him. "Can you do it, Caroline?" If he would ask that of her, to be tough and make it through the fire, the pain, then he must ask the same of himself. He would survive, if only for them.

Hours passed. He had lifted off the *Princeton* at 0600 hours. His watch showed 0400 hours. Twenty-two hours since he'd taken off with his squadron from the carrier deck. He hadn't slept much the night before. He and Roberts had spent hours talking about God and religion. The questions and answers that conversation created had kept Neil up most of the remaining hours, thinking, until early morning. Over forty hours without sleep. His muscles ached. His lungs felt as if they were on fire. He could see the white foam glistening in the moonlight as it lapped in small waves along the beach.

His paddle hit something hard. Coral.

He was on a reef. He lifted himself over the side of the raft and began to walk unsteadily over the bed of jagged coral. It was awkward to stand, let alone walk on the stuff. He stumbled and staggered, pulling the small raft along with him. Several times he fell, cutting his arms and legs on the sharply calcified sea formation. He must have fallen a dozen times before he realized that the shoreline was only fifty yards ahead. One hundred and fifty more steps and he would be on solid ground.

He stumbled onto the beach, falling into the sandy cushion. He lay there, physically drained, unaware that he had let his raft float back out into the surf. He knew that he must move— move into the palm grove a hundred feet or so off the beach. But he couldn't move a muscle. His body wouldn't respond to his commands. Cut, bruised, motionless, but grateful to be alive, he fell into a deep and complete sleep.

Western Union

October 20, 1944
Pasadena, California

Caroline awakened to the pleasant chirping sound of a small bird outside her bedroom window. She wrestled with getting out of bed. For two nights in a row she had dreamed that Neil had come to her. She felt warm, whole, loved. Since little Neil hadn't yet stirred, she could just lie there, listening to the song of the bird. Then it hit her. There, sitting on a ledge, was a small bird—a swallow!

Caroline threw the covers off herself and angrily flung her arms toward the small winged creature. "Shoo—fly away! Shoo—leave!" She rapped on the window with her hand. Then she covered her shivering body with her arms. She was shaken, her hands and feet weak.

It means nothing. Absolutely nothing, she told herself as she walked out of the bedroom and into the kitchen to start a pot of coffee.

It was 8:00 A.M., time for the morning news broadcast. She turned on the Philco and began to work with the water on the stove. The announcer started with war news.

This morning, it was announced, the combined forces of the Allied Pacific Fleet and Armies, under the direction of Gen. Douglas MacArthur, launched attacks against Japanese forces throughout the Philippine Islands. In what has been called the largest naval armada in American history, the Pacific Fleet assembled at dawn, Philippine time, and began to engage the enemy on land and at sea. "Reports of naval air attacks against the capital city of Manila have been confirmed. For more on the latest developments, stay tuned to this CBS radio network."

The seemingly banal chatter and music of advertisements came on the air.

"Dear God!" Caroline cried aloud. Feeling a wave of weakness, she grabbed hold of the kitchen table, easing herself down on the wooden chair. She understood what her anxious feelings had meant. And now, the dream of Neil coming to her, of his hands being cut, of his questioning her if she could do it, as if it meant—

The bird. "It was a sparrow, not a swallow," she told herself. The story her friend had told her—how a swallow had alighted on the window ledge when she washed dishes and how three days later a telegram came, a Western Union telegram, telling her family that her brother had been killed on Guadalcanal. The worst possible news came in Western Union telegrams. Telegrams prefaced by swallows! Caroline put her hands to her head, trying to convince herself that it was all a bad dream—or that she wasn't going crazy.

Caroline felt cold. She crossed her arms and slumped her head down on them. Her breathing was heavy as she sought to regain emotional control. The war. It controlled her life.

The news report came on again.

"People of the Philippines, I have returned!"

The announcer continued. "The voice you just heard was actual radio transmission of words spoken by Gen. Douglas MacArthur as he strode ashore today onto the island of Leyte. His address, in part, carried a message to the Filipino people that he is in personal command at the front and has landed with his assault troops.

"The battle for the liberation of the Philippines commenced earlier yesterday morning with attacks by U.S.–based carrier aircraft of the Fifth and Third Fleets. The planes struck at targets throughout the Philippines as American and Allied troops landed on the southern island of Leyte. The largest naval armada in U.S. history is pursuing what is left of the Imperial Japanese Fleet. There are no reports of casualties at this hour. We will bring you updates of this battle as we receive them. Now for the rest of the news. In Europe today . . ."

Caroline switched off the radio and sat in stunned silence, staring blankly into the living room, chilled by the dark and oppressing feeling coursing through her. The news had been positive enough—so why did she feel this way?

She had been to the theater the Saturday before to watch newsreels. She had to know, to see what her husband was facing. She remembered looking on in tense silence as the camera mounted on the nose of a navy Hellcat fighter recorded the bombing and strafing of enemy ships in the Mariana Islands. She had seen footage of the Battle of the Philippine Sea, or the Marianas Turkey Shoot, as it was also called. American forces decimated Japanese air and naval forces, virtually eliminating them as a viable offensive fighting machine. She instinctively knew that Neil had been engaged in that combat. In fact, she imagined the footage being shown was shot from his plane.

Fear. She never had known such fear in all her life. The pilots and servicemen in the newsreels always smiled, as if they had no fear at all. Or were they just hiding it? Like Neil did. Trying to bury his true emotions and feelings. They seemed to swagger with disdain at the dangers around them.

She recalled the words in the dream so clearly. Neil's words: "The thorns appear to everyone. Can you do it, Caroline?" She didn't have any choice but to handle it. The thorns. They hurt, they cut, they made it so difficult to cling to the rose.

Neil had no idea how long he had been lying there. The water moving over his body and the rays of the morning sun awakened him, along with the sounds of life coming from the jungle that sprang up just a few yards from the beach. He came to long enough to crawl into a nearby grove of trees and brush. The jungle was alive with sounds of every type. The chattering of birds and monkeys mixed with the roar of ocean waves, creating a surreal sense of life—like a dream you couldn't wake from.

Neil opened his life vest's pocket to take out his survival kit. He broke out some crackers and tried to eat them with a dry mouth. He still had his gear, a Colt .45 with two clips of ammo, and the package, his good luck charm and letter from Caroline. He was thirsty, hungry, and needed to get his bearings. Pulling out his compass, he estimated a location based upon his last look at Manila Bay before he hit the water. He guessed that he was on the Bataan peninsula, the same one where MacArthur and his troops had made their last stand some two and one half years before. The place would still be crawling with Japs. And the way things looked, they were not likely to feed and keep him prisoner. No, they would interrogate and then kill him outright; be done with him. On the offense they had been inhumane captors. On the defense certainly they would be no less brutal.

He had to start moving. Taking his coordinates, he decided to head for the mountains, where he might find bands of loyal Filipino guerrilla fighters.

He needed to hold out until the American invasion of Luzon commenced. It was only a matter of time. Weeks, maybe months, but no more than that. The landing in Leyte Island to the south was just the first in a string of liberations. He needed some time; just a little longer, then he could go home. Luzon, after all, was the prize, Bataan a bitter memory for MacArthur. No doubt the general would attack the peninsula soon to pay the Japs back for the brutality they had inflicted on his forces and the Filipino people. No doubt.

He began to trudge west, toward the southern Zambale mountains. There were no trails and the jungle was so thick that it created a stifling humidity mixed with the shadowy darkness from the living canopy overhead. The thickness of the trees blocked the sun but kept the heat in.

It must be 120 degrees, he thought. Sweat poured off him in buckets. He had meandered for hours, in circles maybe. His throat was parched and ached for moisture. He stumbled a few more feet toward a clearing and, utterly exhausted, sat down under a palm tree. Overhead he saw coconuts. They would have moisture. But he couldn't get to them. He didn't have the strength.

It started to rain. The monsoon had come to save him. He looked for a way to scoop the droplets into his mouth. At first he just lay there with his mouth open, letting the kind moisture soothe his parched throat. Then he noticed the water running off the leaves. Eagerly he gathered a large palm frond and positioned it to drain the drops into his mouth. But he couldn't save the water; he had lost his canteen somewhere getting out of his plane. He soaked in all he could, until his exhaustion sent him drifting into unconsciousness.

How long he had been asleep, Neil didn't know. What day it was, he couldn't be sure of. He awakened to the noises of the jungle. His first thoughts were of food and water. He had to kill an animal if he could, then somehow make a fire. If he could just get his hands on the coconuts. The meat and the juice should last him a while. Pondering his dilemma he heard the sound of a click—then a rustling in the bush behind him. He pulled out his Colt .45 and dove for cover—but felt the sharp point of an object in the small of his back. He dropped the gun and turned to face his captor—a diminutive tribesman. The mountain native pulled his spear back and smiled broadly at the lieutenant.

"You American! You American!" he repeated excitedly several times. "Morang! Morang!" The words came as the tribesman thumped himself squarely on his chest to indicate his name. Two other tribesmen, dressed in nothing more than loincloths, appeared from the jungle. They smiled at the American as they chattered among themselves.

"Thirsty . . . Thirsty." Neil made gestures with his hands to his mouth and throat.

"Tirstee . . . Tirstee," the one who held the spear repeated laughingly. Then he was up the tree in a second, dropping coconuts to the ground with a machete. The two others quickly grabbed them and used their machetes to open them for the American.

Neil drank the sweet milk greedily, then began to devour the coconut meat they had pried loose for him. The mountain natives acted delighted, talking and laughing among themselves as Neil concentrated on the fruit.

When they caught his attention again and began to speak, Neil shook his head to indicate he couldn't understand. With gestures they indicated a trail and beckoned Neil to follow them. Then Morang brightened and drew his hand across his throat. "Kill Japs." He thumped himself on the chest. "Kill Japs." He pointed to his two companions, repeating the words: "Kill Japs.

Kill Japs." The small mountain man drew his hand across his throat again to indicate his intentions.

"Okay." Neil slowly rose, drawing his hand across his throat. Then pointing to himself, he smiled to them and said, "American fight."

They all laughed approvingly and went ahead on the trail, motioning him to follow. He hoped they would lead him to other Americans, who might be fighting alongside the Filipino guerrillas in the jungles. He picked up his Colt and other gear and followed them into the thick jungle darkness.

Three days had passed since that morning when the small bird appeared at Caroline's window. No more letters came from Neil. The news from the Philippines was that American forces were winning on land and at sea. There had been one American aircraft carrier, one destroyer, one cruiser, and other smaller American naval vessels destroyed by desperate Japanese kamikaze attempts to forestall the invasion.

She knew that more than a dozen aircraft carriers were attached to a fleet and that there were two fleets engaged in the fighting. She prayed that it wasn't the *Princeton* that had been destroyed, but she couldn't stop imagining just that. No word was almost as bad as hearing the worst.

Caroline tried to dismiss the coincidence of the dreams. Two nights in a row. The sweetest dreams she had known for all the time he had been gone. Then the happenstance of the swallow, or sparrow, appearing at her window. She tried to put it out of her mind.

Yesterday she had gone to Saint Andrew's Cathedral to pray. She wasn't a Catholic, but it was Neil's place of worship and she felt close to him—and to God—when she went there. No answers, no real peace came. But she had to turn to someone. Escorted by little Neil in his stroller, she knocked on Father O'Donnell's door; he answered, looking older than she had remembered.

"Caroline Thomas! Come in! Come

in, child." The white-haired priest gave her a warm embrace. "What brings a good Methodist girl like you to our sanctuary this lovely October morning?" He must have known from the look on her face. Gently he took her by the hand, led her to a chair beside his small worktable that served as a desk.

"I don't know where to go, Father. Or what to do," she offered tearfully.

"What's wrong, child?" He wanted her to tell him.

"Oh . . . I haven't heard from Neil for a while—and this battle that's going on in the Philippines. I know he's there, and—" she couldn't go on.

The old priest came near to her and, kneeling down, let her cry it out on his shoulder. "I understand, I understand, dear," he said softly. "How can I help you feel better? Can we pray together?"

Caroline lifted her head, smiled weakly, and nodded. She struggled to contain the tears.

"Okay, then. You hold on to these beads and pray the words I pray. Then you come back to see me each day until you feel His strength, God's strength."

They began to pray the rosary together. There was a pause, then, the final "Amen." A serene sense of well-being filled the small room. The priest then counseled her, giving her comfort.

"There, now. Come back any time, Caroline, day or night. My door is always open. I will pray for Neil. Look to God, child. Look to him in all your troubles. Please take this." He handed her the crucifix with the prayer beads. "It is identical to the one I gave Neil on his last visit to me."

"Thank you, Father O'Donnell. I feel much better. You'd make a good Methodist, Father."

"And you a good Catholic, child."

Caroline went back home comforted. After putting Neil Junior down for his nap, she retreated to the bedroom to be alone. It was around noon that she began to feel the need to pray. She knelt by the bed, but the words wouldn't come. Just thoughts. Just his words, from the dream.

"Can you do it, Caroline?"

Then came a knock at the door. A cold chill swept through her. She didn't want to answer. If it were regular mail, Mr. Myers would just put it through the mail slot and be on his way. She hadn't wanted to see the postman, not for the last three days anyway.

At the second knock, she slowly rose and headed for the oak-paneled door. She had to do whatever it took, whatever Neil would want her to do.

Squinting through the windowpane, she could make out the shadow of a man. Perhaps it was a package from Neil; perhaps it was a special delivery letter saying everything was okay. Maybe it's not Mr. Myers. She cautiously approached, grasping the doorknob and opening it as if in doing so quickly any bad news would just go away. As it swung open, she could see his back to it.

"Yes, Mr. Myers. What can I do for you?" she voiced weakly, her heart pounding with fear.

He turned around slowly. She could see the strain on his face, the tears gathered in the corners of his eyes. He couldn't speak. He couldn't move. He just looked at her.

"This—" Mr. Myers swallowed hard, trying to finish the sentence. He looked down at the ground, regaining his composure. He held up the Western Union. "This just came in, Caroline. I'm so, so sorry if . . ." He held it out to her with an unsteady hand.

She looked at Mr. Myers, then down at the Western Union telegram with a sense of incredulity. Her mind rejected what was happening. Instead she searched his face for any hint of a bad joke. But he continued to hold the telegram in his outstretched hand.

Suddenly her body felt helpless; her legs seemed to buckle under her. A stinging, white-hot feeling ran through her, making her grip the door for support. Mr. Myers reached out to steady her as she slid slowly to the floor. Letting out a faint gasp for air, she strained to control the emptiness that suddenly enveloped her.

"Caroline! Mrs. Thomas. Come on, honey, let's get you inside."

The postman set his mailbag aside,

gently lifted the sobbing young woman up, and guided her slight, trembling frame to the sofa. She lay back, trying to comprehend what was happening to her. Finally, looking back toward him, she whispered, "Please—please forgive me, Mr. Myers." She wiped away the moisture that coursed down her face, and fought for the courage to receive the telegram from his hand.

"I know how you must feel," offered the gentle voice of her friend. "I'll just leave this here on the coffee table. You should call somebody, and don't open it until they arrive. Okay, sweetheart?" He was looking down at her as she struggled with catching her breath. "I want you to know—if there is anything, anything at all that I can do for you, I will. You'll be all right."

She struggled to respond, but her voice would not come.

Mr. Myers, too, now struggled for control, as if he couldn't come to terms with what awful truth the telegram must hold.

When he spoke at last, his voice was shaky. "I'm sorry, truly sorry, Mrs.

Thomas. Call someone to come over. God bless you, dear." He turned to go to the door. But as he reached for the door handle, he heard her call out to him through a strained, tearful voice.

"I'll be okay. I know it will be all right. Thank you, Mr. Myers."

The postman nodded sadly, then opened the door and left, gently closing it behind him.

Caroline stared at the telegram. "Can you do it?" came the words from the dream. She wanted to sleep, go back to the safety of the dream and hold Neil again. The words pounded in her head like a line from a song, a line or verse that just won't leave until you replace it with another tune.

She reached for the yellow Western Union, fingered it. Then she arose and walked to the wall phone. She put in the call to Richmond 932. The phone was picked up on the other end.

"Hello. Jensens," came the reply.

"Jenny?" asked the emotion-filled voice.

"Yes. Caroline, is that you?"

"Yes. Jenny, can you come over?

And Mom, can she come? Right now? . . . Yes, I'll be fine. Please hurry." Her trembling voice hadn't fooled her big sister.

Caroline hung up the receiver, staggered back over to the sofa. Reaching for the telegram, she slowly opened it.

1234 67 GOVT = WASHINGTON DC A.M.
OCT. 23, 1944
MRS. CAROLINE THOMAS
MARENGO AVE.
PASADENA, CALIFORNIA

THE NAVY DEPARTMENT DEEPLY REGRETS TO INFORM YOU THAT YOUR HUSBAND NEIL THOMAS, LIEUTENANT USN, IS MISSING FOLLOWING ACTION WHILE IN THE SERVICE OF HIS COUNTRY. THE DEPARTMENT APPRECIATES YOUR GREAT ANXIETY BUT DETAILS NOT NOW AVAILABLE. DELAY IN RECEIPT THEREOF MAY BE NECESSARILY EXPECTED. TO PREVENT POSSIBLE AID TO YOUR COUNTRY'S ENEMIES PLEASE DO NOT DIVULGE THE NAME OF YOUR HUSBAND OR SHIP ASSIGNMENT.
VICE ADMIRAL JACOBS,
CHIEF NAVAL ADMINISTRATIVE SERVICES

"He's not dead! They don't know!" Caroline sank to her knees. Coupling her hands together, she offered a prayer: "Dear God, thank you. He's not dead. Missing isn't dead!"

When she looked up with tear-filled eyes, wiping at her stained cheeks with the back of her right hand, the first thing she saw was the hand-carved sign Neil had made remodeling the house: "Belief is the substance of things hoped for, the evidence of things not seen."

The void in the silent room blended with Caroline's whispered prayer. "Thank you, God. Help me to believe."

Forever . . . A Promise to Keep

Lt. Neil Thomas had been with the guerrillas for over three months. He had not yet met up with any other American. He had sent word to the American guerrilla commander of the southern Luzon region, a Colonel Barker, that he was alive and wished to join the main body of the guerrilla force as soon as possible. Whether word had gotten through, he didn't know. He wanted to make his status known, that he was alive, not missing in action. He hoped somehow that Colonel Barker would be able to relay that to the American HQ and that, in turn, Caroline could be notified.

He had become acquainted with the customs of the mountain guerrillas, had earned the right to their respect by participating in several attacks on Japanese patrols and encampments throughout the Bataan region of the southern Zambale mountains.

Ernesto Rios, the young, angry Filipino lieutenant, leader of the company of ninety guerrillas, had sought Neil's approval on their forays against the Japanese. Rios, bent on revenge, justified the brutal way his men would inflict death on the Japanese, whether in battle or if captured. He had learned English serving in the Filipino scouts of the defeated American army four years previous. Rios was fearless in his attacks, keeping his prisoners alive just long enough to extract the information he wanted.

Neil had a hard time with prisoner executions, and Rios knew it. It only pushed the young Filipino harder to show the American pilot that payback to the Japanese was justifiable. Rios would prove to the American that the Japanese got what they deserved.

Then there was young Morang, and his cousins. Morang couldn't be more than seventeen or eighteen years old, Neil had surmised. He and his tribal cousins were the indigenous peoples of the mountains, whose knowledge of the terrain and skills gave the Filipino guerrilla band an added advantage over the Japanese. The three tribesmen had become Neil Thomas's unofficial bodyguards, a duty they discharged with pride. Gradually Neil had learned enough native Tagalog, and had taught Morang and the others enough words in English, that they could reasonably communicate. He was "Tomás" to the guerrillas in the ninety-man company.

"Tomás." Morang gestured with a stick at the flame-cooked wild boar meat dangling from the end. "Eat, Tomás." They were hiding in a cave that overlooked the valley called Sombro.

Neil reached for the meat, irritated by his weakness. He had been surprisingly healthy for the first month and a half; but in January he had contracted first malaria, then dysentery. His weight, and strength, had dropped considerably.

"It will be over soon, Tomás. You'll see. The American army is less than one hundred kilometers down Zig Zag Pass. Japs fighting hard, but we'll kill them and you go home," Rios said.

Rios and his staff officers, Raul Calderas and Pablo Zadillo, eyed the bearded American pilot. They liked him and, like the tribesmen, were sworn to protect him. They would be proud to meet the first American unit to arrive up the road and safely deliver one of their own to them. It would prove their loyalty and gratitude to General MacArthur for returning to the Philippines.

It was February 13th, 1945. The American forces had invaded the main island of Luzon one month earlier. The U.S. Army Sixth Corps was fighting a stubborn enemy, one kilometer at a time, up Zig Zag Pass. The army sought to control the main artery that ran east to west across the top of the

Bataan peninsula, connecting the western coast of Luzon to Manila Bay.

Neil had kept careful diary notes in his flight log that he had managed to rescue from the life vest he'd left on the beach the day he met Morang and the two other tribesmen. By trading his Zippo lighter to a Filipino fighter he had rounded up some paper to keep him on a regular letter-writing schedule. The first thing he would do when he finally joined an American army patrol and got back behind the lines would be to get the packet of daily letters, safely stored in an old .30-cal. ammo box, into the hands of the HQ mail clerk. The Valentine card with the rose Caroline had given him—and which he had carried through it all, repairing it and elaborating on it—he would carry home to her himself as he had promised in the station. He thought that maybe, by March, the letters could arrive—and he prayed that he and the Valentine would not be too far behind them. Caroline would be surprised at what he had constructed from his C-ration box lids.

He pictured his beautiful young wife

and his little son running toward him in the tunnel at Union Station. The dream kept him alive, though the dysentery had sapped his strength. If he could hold out just a little longer, he could make it. He'd get pumped back up with solid American food, be home in a month or so.

He wondered about his shipmates on the *Princeton.* Neil, of course, had no way of knowing about the bomb that sank the carrier on October 24, 1944, just three days after he went down. The *Princeton* had become the only major carrier casualty of the Battle of Leyte Gulf. While the Americans had virtually wiped out the Japanese navy, a new enemy tactic called "divine wind," the *kamikaze*, had gotten through to the task force. Suicide pilots used their planes as manned bombs, with disastrous results for dozens of American warships.

In the case of the *Princeton,* one single, well-placed bomb had caused the death of hundreds of sailors and pilots, and had sunk the mighty carrier. Among the dead were some of Neil's closest comrades. Ensign Roberts was critically injured and shipped stateside. Wilkerson had survived, but lost a leg. Chad Watson, fighter squadron commander, died. Ensigns John Perry, Hickens, Mallory, Phipps—all dead.

He couldn't know it, but a PBY Blackcat rescue plane had radioed back to the *Princeton* about finding Neil's raft floating empty in Manila Bay. He was listed as missing in action; but when the *Princeton* went down, the navy couldn't confirm to his wife whether his raft had been found before or after the sinking of the carrier. The matter wouldn't become clear to Caroline until the injured Ensign Roberts paid a visit to her, that very week, in February 1945.

As Neil lay in the cave, trying to muster strength to make one more patrol with the Filipinos, he remembered the last conversation he and Roberts had, the day before their final mission together back on October 20th.

"Bobby?" Neil had called from his lower bunk.

"Yeah, Skipper?"

"Bobby, I know you're a religious man. Do you practice your religion? You know . . . I mean, do you go to church?"

"Yeah. I guess you could say so," the younger man answered. "Haven't been to church lately," he laughed.

"I don't know if I ever told you, but when I lived with my parents in Ogden I went to your church a few times."

"No, Lieutenant. I didn't know."

"Yeah. My best friend was my next-door neighbor, Dan Oaks. Played a lot of basketball on the church team. Went to dances and stuff."

"No kidding? What was your family doing in Ogden? You're from Pasadena, right?"

"My dad got a transfer from Union Pacific Railroad from LA. Times were tough. It was the depression. You know. It was take the transfer or lose the job. So we packed up and moved."

"That explains it all right," Roberts said.

Neil lay on his back with his hands behind his head. "Bobby, I've got some things on my mind, some things that my priest in Pasadena said to me before I shipped out. You feel like talking?"

"Well, yeah, Skipper. If you do."

"This may sound corny, but I believe in God more now. I mean since I've been out here in the war."

"It doesn't sound corny to me," the twenty-year-old pilot said in a low voice. "I'm glad you said that. I feel the same way."

"Good. I don't want you to think I'm soft. I haven't told anyone why I think I froze that day last month. You remember?"

"Hey, no one holds that against you. You've been out here a long time. No one in the squadron has the record you have. If anybody says anything about it, I'll deck 'em for you."

"You're all right. Thanks, I needed that." Neil chuckled.

They grew serious then, both caught up in silent thought. Neil really wanted to talk about how much he loved his wife. He'd fight and die for her, if he needed to.

"Bobby, let me throw some stuff at you."

"Fire away, Skipper."

For the next three hours the two shipmates discussed deep and troubling theological possibilities about men at war—killing other men. What God would do. Would He take sides?

Near the end of their discussion, Neil propped himself up on his elbow. He wanted one last opinion from his flying buddy. He asked, "What do you believe? What do you down deep really believe life is all about? Tell me what you really think."

"Oh, man, Skipper, that's a tough one. I guess I believe that we all have a unique purpose. That there must be a God. There's got to be more than this. I guess it's about finding peace, peace of mind. Knowing who you are. It's about loving a woman and your kids with a belief that you can be with them forever. Once you know that, the possibility of death doesn't rob you of your peace of mind. Peace in your heart." He stopped and waited. The silence vibrated with deep, meditative thought.

"Peace of mind, huh . . .? Forever." Lieutenant Thomas repeated the words. "Bobby . . . that thing about forever?"

"Yeah?"

"No one should ever make a promise they don't intend to keep. I've always signed my letters to my wife, 'Forever, your loving husband.' You know, so she'll know how important she is, how much she means to me.

"Bobby, don't ever say that word unless you mean it. God in heaven, I do love her. Forever is a promise to keep. Remember that when you have a woman."

"I won't forget it, Skipper. This is the closest I've been to a church in a long time. Thanks."

Roberts's simple faith impressed Neil. "Why don't you say a prayer or something? I'd like it if you would." The embarrassment born of manliness had been abandoned by both navy men hours earlier. Neil knelt by the bunk on the open floor.

Bobby looked down from his top

bunk at his flight leader, then responded to Neil's nod by swinging himself down from the bunk and landing on his knees. Neil watched with respect as Bobby closed his eyes and began. He offered the sign of the cross and listened.

"Father in Heaven, we thank Thee for our lives, our brotherhood, and for all we have, especially our families. God bless them. Please protect them while we are away. Protect us on our missions. We desire to return home. And bless both Lieutenant Thomas and me. Thy will be done, forever, in the name of Thy son. Amen."

"Thanks, Bobby. Don't tell the others about our discussion. I'd like to—well, I'd like to keep it private. I've got some things to sort out." Neil clenched his jaw tight. He felt good, like he'd just bathed, but from the inside out.

Bobby just nodded, shook hands as they looked at each other, and swung himself back up to his bunk.

For a moment Neil couldn't say anything. For the first time in his life he was sure that God knew who he was, where he was, and what he was thinking and feeling. Not that he didn't believe; it was just that now the meaning of a cat-echism Scripture he'd learned as a kid carried power:

> *Where two or more are gathered*
> *in my name,*
> *there shall I be also.*

"We'd better hit the sack, Roberts. It'll be a long day tomorrow."

"Aye, aye, sir."

"Skipper?" Roberts, a few minutes later, asked in a low tone.

"What is it, Bobby?"

"If something happens to me—I mean, if I don't make it back, and you get home, could you call my folks in Salt Lake and tell them—you know, tell them I loved them and tell them I did my duty well. Would you do that for me?"

"On one condition."

"You got it. What?"

"If I don't make it back, you go see my wife, Caroline, in Pasadena. You tell her I said, 'I love you isn't good enough—not for you, Caroline.' Then give my little boy a big hug for me. Agreed?"

"Roger. Agreed, Skipper."

Neil stretched out in the dark, dank-smelling cave. That memory was now three months old. It was turning light outside, and the day was February 14, 1945. The day he should have been home by. He wouldn't make it back to LA's Union Station for his anniversary as he had promised Caroline. "Forever" now had a world of meaning, a meaning he never could have fathomed. He wondered. Would Ensign Roberts be able to keep his word?

Hope

Wednesday, January 21, 1998
Washington, D.C.

I was exhausted by the time my flight landed in Washington, D.C., the night before the *American Diary* interview with Colonel Jackson. But I was anxiously anticipating the next day. Susan had already taken care of my transportation and hotel arrangements, making it easy for me; so I checked in at the lobby, went immediately to my room, and dropped into bed.

I took extra care getting dressed the next morning, wearing a tan wool sport coat over a starched, white open-collar shirt and Docker slacks, then caught a cab to the Smithsonian.

It was a beautiful morning as my taxi pulled up to the entrance of the Air and Space Museum. The sun was shining and the temperature unseasonably warm, already 59 degrees.

Inside, I asked a young woman at the information desk if she could direct me to Colonel Jackson's office. Instead, she offered to announce my arrival, then picked up the phone, notifying his office. She hung up the phone and said he was on his way out, that he wanted to welcome me to the museum in person. I thanked her, then waited, looking around.

Moments later, a tall slender man with closely cropped, graying brown hair walked up to me, his voice bellowing as he held out his hand, "Neil Thomas?"

"Yeah. I mean . . . yes, sir. Colonel Jackson?"

"None other. But please, call me David. It's a pleasure to finally meet you, Neil."

"Likewise," I responded, returning his handshake, a little surprised by his commanding presence and the firm grip he had on my hand.

"Have you seen the museum before?" he asked, immediately putting me at ease. When I told him this was my first trip to Washington, he glanced at his watch and said, "Looks like we might have a few minutes to spare. Why don't I show you around?"

We entered a huge exhibition hall where several planes were displayed, including a World War II P-38 Lightning. I was drawn to it like a magnet. I walked around its fuselage, amazed by the craftsmanship of this sturdy 1940s fighter, then turned to him and said, "I know I've said this before, David, but I want you to know how much I appreciate everything you've done. Your discovery changed my life, and my mother died a happy woman because of it. I don't know if I can ever repay you."

"It's nice to hear that, but you don't owe me anything, Neil. Most men in my position aren't lucky enough to learn more about the history of that conflict by locating a missing war hero. It was an honor, believe me," he said.

I was about to say something else, when a familiar voice cut off the thought.

"Good morning, gentlemen," Susan called out, blowing into the room like a winter storm. "All set?" she asked, smiling at both of us. "I'm sorry to hurry you along, but my crew has two tapings today, so every minute counts."

Colonel Jackson took the lead as we headed back to his office. Along the way, Susan turned to me, giving me a warm smile, and asked if I'd had a pleasant trip. I smiled in return, saying it couldn't have been better, then thanked her again for handling the arrangements.

By the time we arrived, Colonel Jackson's office was just about ready to go. Susan's crew had already set things up and were running a final check on the equipment. I moved to one side of the room, doing my best to stay out of everyone's way.

It soon became obvious that Susan and her crew were seasoned professionals. She invited Colonel Jackson to sit opposite her in one of the upholstered chairs her crew had positioned in front of the wall-length bookcase. In no time at all, the cameras were rolling, and the interview was well underway.

She led in by asking him a few questions about the events that had taken him to the Philippines in the first place. Once he'd warmed up to his story, he turned out to be a great storyteller. You could have heard a pin drop in the room; everyone seemed to be hanging on his every word.

Soon he was talking about the old guerrilla fighters who'd shown him my father's last battlefield, the men who had entrusted him with my father's personal effects, and the amazing gift that ultimately came to my mother and me through his hands.

I was surprised by the emotions stirring in me, as if I were hearing it all for the first time. As he related his captivating experiences, the strong voice softened as he neared the end and I found myself transported back in time. I was meeting Miguel and Morang face to face, seeing the battle scene, then the cave, with my own eyes.

He finished. Susan turned to the camera and smiled, making her final comments with a teaser that promised her audience a "conclusion worth waiting fifty years for." When she glanced at me, a questioning look in her eyes, I gave her a warm smile and nodded my head in approval.

Susan and I chatted with Colonel Jackson while the crew packed up the equipment; then we said good-bye to him at the door of his office. I thanked him again for everything he'd done and promised to keep in touch.

We walked out of the museum together. I held the door open for her and told her how impressed I was with her work. She laughed self-consciously at the compliment, then thanked me in a businesslike tone. But I noticed her face had suddenly flushed. I asked her if she had time for a short walk, maybe a quick lunch.

"I'd like that," she said, in measured enthusiasm. "I knew you'd be leaving this afternoon, so I kept the rest of this morning open. We need to go over the plan for the next three weeks, too. There's still a lot to be done."

"I'm all ears," I said. And eyes, I thought to myself, smiling down at her as we started out toward the mall.

Susan couldn't remember the last time she'd taken a casual stroll with an attractive older man. Now, walking with Neil, she found herself tongue-tied, as if she were a schoolgirl again.

"It's a beautiful day, isn't it?" she said, regretting it immediately. She had a million questions she wanted to ask him, and she'd said something inane about the un-usually springlike weather.

"Couldn't be better," Neil replied sin-cerely.

They were walking up the mall, between the Washington Monument and the Capitol Building. It was the first time since she'd arrived in Washington that Susan had paid any attention to her surroundings. She wanted to take care of business, then talk about something that mattered.

"So listen. I'll be coming back to Califor-nia on the 30th—next Friday. We're going to have two days of shooting. I'll need some footage on the train station, then we'll do the final interview at the house. I'll finish the story before I get there. I really am anxious to get back to it, but my sched-ule's impossible right now."

"I understand—especially now that I've seen you in action," he said. "And I think you'll find it won't be a waste of your time, when you do get around to it."

"I don't doubt that now." She looked him directly in the eyes, wanting him to see her earnestness, then found herself opening up to him. "You know, this really is nice, walking like this. I'm afraid I never take the time."

"Why not?" Neil asked.

"Oh, I don't know. Priorities. Work. What seems most urgent at the moment. I've always thought it was my career, but that doesn't seem like enough anymore. I've got everything I thought I wanted, but it seems like something's missing sometimes." Susan stopped, then, her eyes shifting to the ground, suddenly became aware that her protective shell was cracking.

"I'll tell you what," Neil said, as if he could sense her discomfort. "Why don't you take a break when you come out next week? I've got to pack some more of my mother's things Saturday morning, and get the living room ready for the interview, but you could meet me there—make sure the room looks okay. I'm free after that, and I can show you around town. You know, some of the places in the story. It could be business *and* pleasure," he finished lightly.

"Sounds great," Susan said, smiling, realizing her stomach was fluttering at the thought of a leisurely afternoon alone with him. She also felt disappointed somehow, that he'd said he was still packing. She couldn't bear to think of him leaving that beautiful old house to strangers, and couldn't resist saying something. "Neil, are you really sure you want to sell your mother's house? I mean, it just seems like such a shame . . . it's got so much character and history."

"Yeah, I've given it a lot of thought. If I kept it, I'd want to move in. My kids are almost grown, and I just don't see myself rattling around in there alone. It feels so empty now."

Susan could see he was drifting away, thinking about his wife and his mother. She kicked herself silently, then tried to brighten the mood by asking about his kids.

He smiled, reached into his back pocket, and proudly took out a photo. "They're dying to meet you . . . I've told them all about you."

Susan didn't ask Neil what he'd said to them—about her—she preferred to imagine. It had been a perfect day so far, and she didn't want anything to change that. She didn't want their time together to end, but she'd made up her mind to spend the rest of the day reading his story. And she had so much to think about.

She glanced up at him, smiling. "You must be proud."

Susan turned the key to the door of her townhouse overlooking Chesapeake Bay and was immediately met by her feline roommate, Daisy. Setting her attaché aside, she picked her up and stroked her soft mane.

"You hungry, Daisy? Come on, let's eat." She walked to the fridge and pored fresh milk in the cat's tray and then threw herself on the sofa to relax and think. She pored over the day in her mind wondering how she had come to lose the control she had so carefully cultivated over the years.

She had said good-bye to Neil earlier in the afternoon followed by an interview at the Capitol Building with a congressman on the status of the current budget crisis. She had found the congressman both dull and boring compared to the man she had spent the morning with. She remembered looking right through him to the mall in the distance and seeing Neil's face.

Neil possessed a strong looking exterior, a face that suggested control, poise and purpose. A gentleman who was truly gentle, he had captivated her. He made the powerful congressman seem small and impotent of character by comparison.

Frustration mixed with her attraction for him. She was a career-path woman, he was a family man. She was in her early thirties, he was in his early fifties. She was consumed with business, he was consumed by solitary meditations. Her daily walk was hectic, fast paced. His was measured, calm, laid back.

Could he fit into her world? Would she fit into his? Susan gazed over at her attaché. The story inside seemed to beckon her. She was falling in love—in love with the old-fashioned tale of romance and devotion between Caroline and Lt. Thomas. And at the center of it all was Neil and a hope. A sincere hope she could sort out the rattling confusion shaking up her well-ordered world.

She went for the story and returned to her special reading spot—the leather lounger situated by the picture window overlooking the bay. She began to read.

February 14, 1945
Union Station, Los Angeles, California

Ens. Bobby Roberts got off the Union Pacific train from San Diego and strode down the concrete ramp at track twelve. He entered the tunnel and headed toward the main lobby, stopping at gate G to confirm his next call for Union Pacific 101 with destination to Salt Lake City. He had just arrived back in the U.S. one week earlier aboard a hospital ship that had docked in San Diego. He had recovered from the burns, cracked ribs, and gash to the head he had suffered months earlier. When the *Princeton* had been hit and sunk in the Battle of Leyte Gulf, he'd received more than physical wounds. He'd seen his friends dead and dying on a smoking carrier deck, and those wounds had not yet healed.

Bobby worked his way through the crowds of departing servicemen and their families toward the waiting area lobby. He was on a special mission today. He had a promise to keep. He'd promised Lieutenant Thomas he would visit his wife and son with a special message from him if Lieutenant Thomas hadn't made it back yet. Bobby had written the words down on a piece of paper so he would have them exact. He had no way of knowing whether Neil was alive or dead, but he inwardly believed the skipper had made it to shore. He was there, today, to offer that hope to Thomas's wife.

Roberts mused on the character of Lieutenant Thomas. He had known strong men before. His own parents were from a long line of self-reliant and hardy pioneering families that helped settle the Rocky Mountain valleys. He had worked side by side with his father, clearing farmland in the Salt Lake Valley as a boy and young man. Things had been scarce and times were hard, but he could always count on his father. Grant Roberts was a man full of strength and energy. The work ethic personified, he seemed to be able to make the impossible possible.

Ensign Roberts had lived an isolated life back then. Then, when the world was a small town and his whole view was deeply embedded in his religious roots, life was simpler. And now, he had been out in a world at war and had met other men, strong men. They were men he could count on with his life— who could seem to take the impossible, like his father, and turn it around into a positive outcome. Men like Lt. Neil Thomas.

If anyone could tackle a life-threatening challenge, that man would be Lieutenant Thomas. He was strong, quick-thinking, and had a courage that made it possible for him to fly into enemy fire. He also possessed an uncommon faith in God. He recalled his last conversation with him aboard ship. The feeling—the bond of brotherhood— had been so strong during their talk that he was sure his life and that of

Lieutenant Thomas were in God's hands.

The brotherhood and trust he felt for Neil had developed quickly. He had needed that kind of leadership, and Roberts felt he owed his life to his flight leader. He knew that the Skipper would die for any of his men. He wished he had been able to search for him. He would have flown over every speck of ocean looking for his downed commander. If only he could have—if only the carrier hadn't been hit. If only he hadn't been sidelined from the war. At least now he could keep his last promise to the man he so deeply respected.

Confirming his next train connection for 2100 hours, 9:00 P.M., Roberts determined that he could get to Pasadena by taxi and have plenty of time to visit with Thomas's wife and son before needing to board his train for Salt Lake. As he headed into the waiting area lobby he checked his watch against the clock on the south wall by the patio area. It was 1300 hours, 1:00 P.M. Habit. Pilot's habit. Precision and timing were the difference between life and death in an air battle, and time was something he appreciated even more now.

He passed by hundreds of servicemen with their wives and girlfriends. The Los Angeles Union Station reminded him of home, in a way. Union Pacific Station on South Temple and Fourth Street West, in Salt Lake, was always packed the same way: couples saying their last good-bye before separating for an uncertain future, and parents tearfully waving to their sons headed off to war. Places were different but the people were the same. He noticed the high ceiling with its massive rafterlike beams and the dark stained wood-paneled walls that surrounded the room, giving it a feeling of largeness. He wondered if the expansiveness of the rooms could ever offer enough space for the emotions that filled a place like this.

He picked up his duffel bag and headed toward the main doors on Alameda Street to catch a taxi. Following the throng heading out through the center of the large cathedrallike halls, he noticed a young woman passing him with the crowds that headed in the opposite direction—toward the departure gates. She sparked a recognition in him he couldn't immediately place. He had seen that face before, but he felt sure he had never met her. He dropped his bag on the highly polished tiled floor and worked his way back through the crowds until he had caught up with her.

"Excuse me, ma'am," he said, tapping her on the shoulder. She stopped and turned around, staring at him with an emotionless, blank look. An energy showed from an otherwise beautiful face that he sensed could be captivating, if the woman were happy.

"Yes?" the young lady answered.

"Excuse me, I know we don't know each other, but—well, you look so familiar, and I—"

She cut him off. "Look, I'm married. If this is what I think it is, I'm not interested."

"Oh, no—no. That's not it. Please forgive me. I thought you might be—well . . ." An awkward pause followed.

"You must be on your way to meet your husband. I'm sorry." Roberts turned to head back toward Alameda Street and the taxis.

"Wait," she called. The young woman wore a flower-patterned dress, her petite frame belying her strength. She carried herself gracefully, digni- fied, with poise. Her auburn hair was neatly put up in a bun, and her brown eyes, though sad, could beguile any man—under different circumstances. She walked toward the young navy pi- lot and stopped, looking at the gold wings on his uniform.

Unabashedly, she stared. Her eyes filled with tears and a small cry es- caped from her throat. "You're a navy pilot," she exclaimed in a soft, trem- bling voice. "Welcome home," she whispered. "I'm sorry I was so sharp with you." She searched her purse for a handkerchief, the one her husband had given her the year before. "My hus- band—I don't know if—when—he's coming home. I just came down here in hopes. He left one year ago, and it's our anniversary. I'm more than a little upset. Anyway, I'm sorry I was rude."

As she struggled to finish offering her apology, a smile crossed the lips of the young navy pilot. She wondered why he was taking time with her and her story anyway, and she was embarrassed at his smile. He just didn't get it, she thought.

"Caroline?"

She looked at him, startled, her gaze questioning, searching his face, to know who it was addressing her by name.

"Are you Caroline Thomas?"

"Yes," came the carefully posed response. "Have we met?"

"Not officially," he replied, extending his hand. "My name is Bobby Roberts, Ens. Bobby Roberts. I've seen your picture many times, on the wall of my quarters aboard ship—the cabin I shared with your husband, Neil."

Caroline let out a faint gasp and put her hand to her mouth. She stared at him, too weak to respond.

He reached out to support his shipmate's wife. "Hey, whatcha say we take that table over there?" He pointed over at a table in the café that was being cleaned by a busboy. "You won't believe this," he continued as he led her through the door, "but I was just headed to catch a taxi to Pasadena in hopes of visiting with you when I noticed you walking by. I've got some information that may be of help to you."

Her face was a portrait of confusion and hope. He offered her a seat, pulling it away from the table and scooting the chair in when she had settled into it. He took a chair opposite her. There was a momentary awkwardness as he sought for a way to begin.

"Where's my husband?" Caroline asked finally, breaking the silence.

Looking into her sad brown eyes, remembering the man—it was almost more than Roberts could take. His mouth struggled to form the words. He fought to restrain the emotions welling up inside him, emotions he didn't want breaking the surface of his carefully controlled manhood. He cleared his throat and took a deep breath as he searched for the words.

"He was alive, the last time I saw him, ma'am. What did the navy tell you?"

She quickly dug into her purse and pulled out two telegrams. An anxious, hopeful look filled her face as she handed them to him.

He read intently. "This is it? This is all they told you?"

"Yes," came the faint reply.

Ensign Roberts shook his head. "I was with him on his last flight."

"When?"

"October 20th. The start of the Philippine invasion. We attacked Clark Airfield and Manila. We lost a couple of planes. Your husband's plane took a hit from antiaircraft fire over Manila. He was one darn good pilot, Mrs. Thomas, and an even better man."

"Thank you. But, I need to know. Was he hurt? Did his plane crash? What happened?"

The questions came rapidly as she leaned over the table, hungry for answers.

"Well, you know how the first telegram listed him missing in action as of October 21, 1944?"

"Yes."

"The second telegram seems to add confusion by saying he was reported missing after the *Princeton* had been sunk. He never made it back to the *Princeton* after his plane was hit over Manila. It was like the first telegram said. He actually became missing after he ditched his plane in Manila Bay."

"Where in Manila Bay? How? Did he survive going down?" She searched Ensign Roberts's face for any clue, any nuance that could offer hope.

Roberts's fists tightened. He fought for composure against the sudden rush of emotion that swept over him. His mind was being carried back to a moment frozen in time. He could picture the skipper with his thumbs-up sign climbing into the life raft. He remembered feeling like he had abandoned him as he wagged his wings to let him know he had made the May Day call. It was a hopeless, gnawing feeling. He had left a friend behind to possibly die, and there wasn't a thing he could do about it.

"I'm sorry, Mrs. Thomas." His voice was thick with emotion. "I had to leave him—and then all the men aboard the *Princeton,* good men, who died. I thought I had better control of my feelings. Just a minute . . ." He swallowed hard, trying to clear the tight feeling that was squeezing his throat shut.

"It's okay. I can wait." She reached across the table and tenderly touched his hand. She had waited this long. Another minute wouldn't make a difference. It warmed her to know that Neil had generated that kind of respect from the men he served with.

The waiter came to the table. "What will you have?"

Ensign Roberts gestured to Caroline.

"I'll have a coffee, black, with sugar."

"A Coke. Ice cold," Roberts said.

"Coming right up." The waiter jotted it down and walked away.

Caroline looked at her husband's navy comrade and waited. She was anxious, but decided not to push. Roberts was suffering enough. She could see he was looking for the words in which to tell her something important.

"Well . . ." Roberts cleared his throat again. "Like I was saying, after his plane got hit, he told me to take over. We had lost one guy, a new guy—Martinez. One of the other planes, Wilkerson's, had taken some hits and he was nursing his Hellcat back to the carrier. Your husband wasn't wounded—at least he said he wasn't. His plane was shot up pretty bad, though. He knew he couldn't get it back to the carrier and had only two choices. One was to bail out over the island of Luzon and take his chances of getting captured by some angry Japs or ditch in Manila Bay. At least in the bay there was a good chance a rescue plane or a sub could pick him up."

"So there was no way for him to get back to the *Princeton*?"

"No, ma'am. No way. His engine froze up."

"How did he get out of his plane?"

"Well, he made a joke out of it."

"Sounds like Neil," Caroline replied, more animated now. She was feeling

more positive. These were the first answers she had received in four months.
"What did he say?"

"Well," he asked if I knew what two
things fell out of the sky. Roberts
grinned. "I said, 'Yeah, fools and bird—'
well, you know."

Caroline couldn't believe that her
tears could now be coming from laughter. They laughed together as the
waiter brought their order. "I love him,"
she whispered fiercely as she remembered his humor and the wonderful
days they had had together.

"Thank you," Roberts acknowledged
to the waiter. "Neil didn't think it was
such a good idea to jump out over the
island with all the Japs we had just
bombed and strafed gunning for us, so
he decided to ride the plane down. He
did a textbook belly landing in Manila
Bay."

"He went down in the ocean, and he
was okay? You saw him?"

"Yes. He performed a classic tail
drag and skimmed across the water to
a stop. I radioed to him and he called
back that he was all right and getting

into his life raft. Then, as I circled over-head, I watched him climb out of his cockpit and onto the wing. He inflated the raft and got in. I didn't leave until I saw him give me the thumbs-up sign. I wagged my wings to let him know I had radioed in a May Day call and that the cavalry, a search party, was on its way to rescue him. He was alive and okay the last time I saw him."

"But if he was alive, and you called for a rescue plane—why? What happened to him?"

"The weather turned bad. It was a stormy afternoon and night. The PBY, called a Blackcat—it's a rescue plane—well, it couldn't find him in all the rain and cloud cover. The next day they went out again and spotted a life raft floating in the surf near the shoreline of the Bataan peninsula. They searched the area and didn't see any sign of him."

"So they didn't keep trying? Did they just give up?"

"No. They went out for two more days. Then our ships got attacked pretty good; the *Princeton* went down, and the PBY crew was lost at sea. The navy knows less than I do about this. I didn't know that they had the information so sketchy. I'm sorry, Mrs. Thomas. I would have written personally."

"I understand, Mr. Roberts."

"Please, call me Bobby."

"Okay, Bobby." Caroline stared into her coffee cup, as if an answer could come from it—an answer to a nagging question. Then she looked up and proposed the question plaguing her. "Bobby? Do you think there's hope? I mean—do you think he could be alive?"

"I do. I think Lieutenant Thomas made it to shore. He was a tough man. He was stubborn and wanted to make it back. Mrs. Thomas—Caroline—if anyone can make it, that person would be your husband."

"I know," she replied. She continued to stare into the blackness of her coffee cup. "Bobby?" She looked at him again. "What would happen to him if he made it to shore—if he were still alive?"

"Well, there are a lot of Americans hiding out in the jungles with the Fili-

pino guerrillas. The Filipinos have res-
cued other pilots, I'm sure. If he made
it to shore, I'm certain he found a way
to locate the guerrillas and wait out the
war with them. He's a fighter, Caroline.
I wouldn't want to be the Jap who tried
to capture him." He meant well by saying it, but sensed that he had just
painted a new picture of worries for the
young wife of his friend. The picture
was one both of hope and anxiety.

"Thank   you,   Bobby."   Caroline
squeezed his hand.

"It's the least I could do. He saved
my life. He helped get me through
some pretty tight spots. He loved you
very much, Caroline. You need to
hope, to hold on and to pray."

She looked at him in amazement.
She thought of Father O'Donnell. It
sounded like him, like something he
would say to her. Maybe the prayer she
offered that morning at Saint Andrew's
Cathedral was being answered now.
Maybe Bobby was sent to answer her
plea. There was silence as they both
reflected on the events that had
brought them together today.

THE LAST VALENTINE   215

Bobby finally spoke. "I feel a little guilty, Caroline. I don't understand how God chooses who lives and who doesn't. I keep thinking of all those men on the *Princeton.* Pilots aren't supposed to die on the carrier. They're supposed to go down doing their duty, if their time is up. Up in the air, flying, I mean. Maybe. Well, I was just thinking—it's kind of a crazy idea, but— maybe God spared your husband the fate of the rest of the squadron. Maybe He let him live by having him shot down before the *Princeton* could be sunk and possibly take his life like it did so many of the others. I know this might sound way out on a limb, but maybe God has saved him for another mission, in a strange sort of way, by having him go missing. Do you understand what I'm trying to say?"

"I think I do," she responded with a faint smile and an expression that bore witness to her gratitude. Caroline didn't want to leave. She didn't want the closeness to Neil that she was feeling to end. She wondered if there wasn't something more. She turned again to the young pilot as he sat there, quietly sipping his drink and staring off into the crowds of passing soldiers. "Bobby?"

"Yes, ma'am?" His gaze went back to the table and to the face of his friend's wife.

"Bobby, did Neil say anything else? I mean, was there any message he might have given you, for me?" She looked hopeful, hungry for signs of the possibility of his survival.

Ensign Roberts perked up. "I almost forgot. I promised to give you a message if anything—well, if he couldn't make it back before I did, he asked me to give you a special message. I wrote it down so I wouldn't forget it." He reached inside his shirt pocket and pulled out the slip of paper. "Here it is: 'Love isn't good enough, not for you, Caroline.'"

Caroline smiled, then looked away, biting into her lip, then she said, simply, "Thank you."

She recalled her dream, the two nights he had come to her. Those words, "Can you do it, Caroline?" kept echoing in her mind.

No matter how long it took, no matter how many Valentine Days or wedding anniversaries passed, she would wait for him. She would tend to their home and garden. He would return to her.

In the dream, he had one more mission before he could come home to her. He was missing, not dead. "Missing isn't dead," she whispered to herself under her breath. She would wait . . . and she would hope.

Valley of Shadows

Friday, January 30, 1998
Pasadena, California

Susan checked into the Pasadena Marriott a little after three on Friday afternoon, looking forward to a long nap. She was delighted to see that the smog blanket had lifted and the mountains were crystal clear in the unfiltered Southern California sun. It had been a long noisy flight, and she'd given up trying to read. If she could sleep for an hour, she thought, she'd have the rest of the evening to relax in her room and finish Neil's story.

As she unlocked the door of her suite and stepped inside, dropping her attaché case on the floor of the foyer, the fragrance of roses assailed her senses. An ivory vase was sitting on the small table, filled with at least a dozen red roses in full bloom.

She knew immediately where they'd come from and hurried to open the card.

Welcome back to Pasadena. The roses are a "thank you" for all you've done. They're Royals—they remind me of you.
Neil

A feeling of warmth swept through her. She hurried to the phone and dialed his number.

"Neil," she said when he answered, "this is Susan. I just found the flowers and I wanted to thank you. They're beautiful!"

"I thought they might brighten your hotel room," he said. "They're prize winners, grafts from the originals my mother and father planted."

"From that wonderful rose garden," she responded. "I'm looking forward to seeing it again tomorrow. What time shall I come by?"

"I want to make sure I've got everything ready. Let's say around two o'clock?"

"Perfect. I'll see you then."

Susan hung up the phone, then lingered by the window for a moment, staring blindly at the street outside, confused by her feelings. She didn't want to wait until tomorrow to see him. She desperately wanted to believe the love his story told of could really exist between people, and maybe it had between Caroline and her lieutenant. But Neil was the only man Susan had ever met who might make her believe—and he was still in love with his wife.

She sighed, pulling herself out of her thoughts. She needed that nap if she was going to read.

February 14, 1945—1200 hours
Zig Zag Pass, Bataan peninsula,
Philippines

"Tomás!" Rios called. "Japs coming down ridge. Maybe one hour. We finish them off. We go in five, ten minutes."

Filipino guerrilla commander Ernesto Rios looked into the cave where downed U.S. Navy pilot Lt. Neil Thomas, Sr., sat hunched over a small makeshift wood table. The American was putting the finishing touches on the elaborate foldout he'd built into Caroline's homemade Valentine card.

"Yeah. Sure. Just a minute more, Ernesto." Lieutenant Thomas coughed weakly. Valle de Sombros—the Valley of Shadows—was a long way from Pasadena . . . from home, he thought. He just wanted to make sure—make sure, if anything happened to him today, Caroline would know. If something happened—if the worst happened—then she would know his last thoughts were of her. It was their wedding anniversary, not to mention the day he promised he'd be home for her one year earlier. He hurried as he folded the carton board C-ration box conscripted to enhance the Valentine, and put it neatly beneath the letters he had written.

"Ernesto!" Neil's tone was muffled. "Ernesto, I need to speak to you."

"Yeah? What you want, Tomás?"

"Can you make me a promise?" He knew his voice showed the strains of sickness.

"Sure, Tomás. No sweat."

"Good. This card that I always carry in my pocket, and these letters"—he pointed to the metal ammunition box where he stored the letters intended for Caroline—"If something happens to me today, will you make sure an American officer gets this box?" Neil looked up to Ernesto from his seated position on the dirt floor of the cavern.

"Yeah, sure. No sweat, Tomás." He reached down and put his hand on the scruffy-looking bearded American's thin shoulder. "Nothin' gonna happen to you today, Tomás. We set trap, kill enemy, Americans come, and you go home. No sweat. We gotta go. Just a couple minutes more. I wait for Morang and then we go."

"Thanks, Ernesto. They'll make you general someday." Both men laughed at the remark.

Neil held up the tattered picture of his wife and newborn son. He took one last hard look before he joined the guerrillas in the ambush on the Japanese soldiers closing in.

His tour in the Pacific would have been up by now. He had over one hundred combat missions logged in his flight diary on the day his plane had been shot down over Manila Bay three and one half months earlier. He was now eligible to be rotated home.

"I love you, Caroline, little Neil," he whispered to the picture. In the dim light of the cave, Neil Thomas smiled.

His kid. He had never held his little boy, never kissed his cheek, never felt the grasp of his boy's tiny hand on his index finger. The hours ahead would determine if he ever would.

He pulled the special card out of the box, the one that went with him on every mission. It had survived with him, gotten badly soaked through the dark night in the raft when his plane was downed in Manila Bay—the card with Caroline's words of love and the crushed red rose from their garden. It had pulled through to comfort him now. Touching the tattered card and the remaining petals was as good as touching home. She would be pleased to see what he had built to protect her rose. He raised it to his face to see if the faint scent of perfume somehow magically would be there for him. It was. Or he imagined it was. And he saw her face again. He watched himself pull Caroline's lips up to his and recalled the emotions of parting that day one year before.

Gently he placed the black-and-white photo in the envelope with the Valentine card, and put them into the ragged pocket of his shirt. Buttoning the top of the pocket he tried to quiet his mind for whatever awaited him.

The thudding of artillery fire sounded in the distance, awakening Neil to the fact that the American Sixth Army was slowly but steadily working its way up Zig Zag Pass from the coast. He reckoned it was maybe fifty to sixty kilometers away.

"Tomás! Morang coming. We go. Get ready," Rios called from the mouth of the cave.

Neil quickly fastened the ammo box

lid securely closed. His letters were stored inside, the card and photograph secure in his pocket. Now if he could just get them into the hands of a postal clerk when the army pushed through to their position.

The diminutive native scout appeared in silhouette at the mouth of the cave. He was out of breath. Neil watched as the tribesman carried on a conversation with Rios in Tagalog. Then the leather-skinned tribesman came over to Neil to see him one last time before the battle. He could see that the American pilot was still weak from dysentery and suffering the ravages of malaria. Neil had remained seated on the floor of the cave, capturing every possible second of rest before following Rios out and into the ambush location.

"Tomás! Japs come!" Morang was still breathing heavily as he hurried into the cave. "Go home. Okay, Tomás? Americans come. Japs—we—" He drew his hand across his throat. He knew exactly how sick his American friend was. He wanted to show he cared.

"Yeah, Morang. Maybe this last fight; then I go home." Neil coughed. In this dank and musty cavern the air carried a sickening scent that made it hard to breathe.

"Morang fight. Tomás no fight." The teenage native motioned with his hand. "Go home, okay?" Morang was doing his best to sound reassuring.

Neil smiled weakly at his friend's effort to be comforting and reached out to shake the small hand Morang extended to him.

"Okay. We go now!" Rios exclaimed.

Neil reopened the lid of the green metal .30-cal. ammunition box. Carefully he removed a shiny metal object. Snapping the lid shut, and double-checking its waterproof seal, he called Rios over to show where he was wedging the box into the crevice behind a boulder. Rios nodded as Neil placed another flat rock over that. He wanted his letters and effects kept safe, just in case.

Rios, impatient to leave, tugged at Neil's sleeve. "We go now."

"Rios, please. Will you tell Morang why I hid this box? That it's very important for you or him to get it to an American officer if something—you know, if I don't make it."

Rios called Morang over and rapidly repeated Neil's instructions to him. Neil pointed to the boulder behind him by the wall of the cave.

"No sweat, Tomás. No Japs . . ." He indicated death in the familiar sign language Neil had come to understand. "Tomás go home. Morang say no sweat."

Rios gave a quick command to Morang in Tagalog and the young tribesman hurried back to Neil with his hand outstretched.

"Tomás, you take." He held out a hand-carved comb made from some sort of wood, possibly bone. A gift for his American friend. He beamed proudly as Neil accepted it, then extended his hand to shake with Neil.

"Here, Morang. Come here." Neil motioned to the young mountain native to help him up. In his hand was his small pocketknife. He had stored it with other personal effects he felt he wouldn't be needing any longer now that the American army was only miles away. It was the most precious thing he could find to give to the mountain native who had saved his life more than once.

Morang smiled as he took the gift from the American's hands. He reassured Neil again by hand gestures not to worry. "No sweat, Tomás." And with that, he stood stiffly erect and offered a salute, which Neil willingly obliged in return.

"Be careful, my friend," Neil called as he watched Morang hurry from the cave to take up his advance position in the jungle. Rios was busy giving last-minute instructions to another guerrilla fighter who had suddenly appeared. All Neil had to do now was hold out with his Filipino comrades, forty-eight hours tops. He was encouraged, but jittery. The old gnawing feeling had come back. The same one he'd felt on the carrier deck the morning of his last mission. The same one he'd felt at Union Station, leaving his wife one year earlier to the day.

Neil wished he could just lie down and go to sleep, go to sleep until the army arrived. But he couldn't. He couldn't let his Filipino friends down. Not after all they had done for him. He had to accompany them on this mission. He just had to hold out for a few hours, make it back to the safety of this cave. He took in a deep breath of the musty air. It made him cough again.

The gangly Filipino guerrilla leader was calling from the mouth of the cave. "Tomás, we go now. Japs on ridge. Trap set. We hurry."

"Right, no sweat, Ernesto." Neil coughed. "Just a few seconds more alone. Okay, Rios?"

"Yeah, sure, but hurry." Rios crouched to scan the valley with his binoculars. They would descend to the ambush site through thick jungle foliage below the rocks and be at the bridge in a couple of minutes. The Japanese were still caught on the far side of the river making their way down the hill through the thick jungle, which obscured them from a clear view of the bridge and the guerrillas' cave hideaway.

Neil pulled out his crucifix that hung loosely with his dog tags on the chain around his neck. It had been tucked inside his ragged shirt. He held it up to the dim light penetrating the opening of the cave. He rubbed his thumb across the top of it and felt the crown of thorns on the figurine on the cross. The crown. It held a world of meaning for him now. Pulling it down to his lips, he kissed it and fell to his knees to pray. Bowing his head, he whispered the Lord's Prayer.

> *Our Father, who art in Heaven,*
> * hallowed be thy name.*
> *Thy kingdom come, thy will be*
> * done*
> *On earth as it is in Heaven.*
> *Give us this day our daily bread,*
> *And forgive us our trespasses*
> *As we forgive our trespassers.*
> *And lead us not into temptation*
> *But deliver us from evil.*

Then he continued:

"Dear God, if You can hear me, I want to ask something . . ." He paused, remembering the simple and direct prayer that his flying buddy Ensign Roberts had offered all those months before on the night before his last flight. The simple prayer had stirred him then and he remembered being sure God had heard it. He needed him now.

"I need to pray for some special things today. I want to go home now. Please protect me and this group of soldiers, my friends. Help me make it through this battle and get home to Caroline and my little boy. Please let me keep the promise I made to Caroline, to come home to her.

"I promise to seek Your will the rest of my life. I just . . .I just want to make it back home. But, God, if I don't—if it's not Your will that I do . . ." He choked on his words, coughed, then continued. "Dear God, please let my wife get these letters if something happens to me—so that she will know. So she'll know how much I loved her. And, please? Please . . ." Neil's weakened voice broke with emotion.

"If this is the final time she receives something from me, let this last Valentine that she gave me reach her. To show her that I've kept it safe for her. That I've improved it, that I love her. It's all I'm asking. Amen."

Neil wiped the moisture from his face with the back of his hand. Then he slowly raised himself to his feet.

"No time to lose. We go now, Tomás," Rios called from the mouth of the cave.

"I'm coming, Ernesto. No sweat," he responded. Neil pulled out his Colt .45, checked the ammo clip, and tightened the rope that held the rotting holster to his trouser belt. He looked back one last time to make sure the ammo box with the letters was securely stored behind the small boulder.

A strange feeling of calm stifled the anxiety he had felt earlier. Maybe God would answer his prayer. Maybe he could make it back home. Or maybe . . . just maybe, Caroline would find out what had happened to him. Maybe she would know. She would get his letters and know how much he loved her as she held the last card he would have to write from the desperation of a dirty war . . . their last Valentine.

"Japs want the valley and the high ground. We let 'em in, then we spring trap. Like a rat to lose its head," Rios said from the mouth of the cave as he looked back at Neil.

Neil quickly undid the sidearm holster from the rope belt and strapped his .45 over his shoulder. He had lost so much weight it was hard to keep the holster up around his waist.

"Kill lots of damn Japs today, Tomás," Rios commanded.

The smile Neil flashed back was more like a grimace. He was tired. Sick and tired. His uniform was in shreds, a rope replaced his belt to hold his ragged pants up, his boots were cracked and falling apart, his feet suffered from jungle rot, he hadn't shaved in three months. He had long ago ceased to be excited about war or killing enemies.

He was hungry for real food and his spirit was worn down. But he needed to show his approval to the aggressive Filipino. He was grateful. They were doing their duty and he was alive because of them.

He made the sign of the cross. "Do it for Caroline and little Neil," he said to himself as he followed Rios out of the cave.

"This way." Rios motioned. They started down the jungle path that led to the river. Rios spoke in low tones. "Japs coming over the ridge. I sent Morang out with his boys to keep track of them. The Japs want to take the pass here at the footbridge. It is a strong defensive position for them, and they could hold the Americans up for weeks. Many lives will be lost if they do that. We kill 'em today. No sweat, Tomás."

"Right. No sweat," Neil answered back. He was struggling to keep up with Rios as they made their way down the slippery trail through the jungle foliage. They moved toward the rocks that provided good cover near the road and the footbridge that paralleled it.

"See? The bridge over the Rio Sombro washes out during the rain. So the Japs think they come and take the footbridge and hold both sides of the river. Then they think they take those cliffs above the narrow pass, on our side, near the cave. They know the valley is too small for planes. The mountains high and no space for them to fly, so they think they hold out here. It's a good idea, but we are already here. We kill 'em all."

Rios had pointed out all of the strategic points where he had stationed his men so that they could cut down the Japanese from ambush once the enemy decided to cross the bridge. He had, indeed, created an excellent trap.

"Good job, Ernesto. They'll make you a general someday." Neil whispered as he did his best to muffle his cough.

The Filipino responded with a broad smile. "You stay here. Men everywhere look out for you. The Americans, they come today, maybe tomorrow. You see. Then they make you admiral." He chuckled at his remark and left to take up a command position closer to the bridge.

Neil observed the setting. It was almost twelve noon. The high mountains still cast a shadow over the valley. It was only at high noon that the sun offered any real light to the jungle floor and road, which crossed the small but treacherous river in the narrow defile. *Not much of a valley*, he thought.

He could clearly see that the Japanese could hold up the advancing Americans for days, maybe even weeks, if they controlled this spot. It was exactly as Ernesto said. It could cost a lot of American lives. They were lucky to have secured it before the Japanese did. Now he just had to hold on until the cavalry arrived.

The footbridge was made out of thick hemp rope. The locals had hewn wood steps from split logs tied together, making it a single-file crossing. The footbridge straddled the river just above the place where it dropped off in a breathtaking one-hundred-foot fall.

The sound of the water cascading to

the frothing pool below and the peaceful jungle scene with its verdant growth and intermittent bird calls belied the violence that was about to take place here. The rope bridge crossed the river about twenty meters south of the washed-out wooden bridge on the road. The Japs would have to try to cross here. They had no other choice.

Raul Calderas came up from behind Neil, startling him. "Tomás, you okay?"

"Not anymore. You just about gave me a heart attack, Calderas."

Calderas flashed the whitest teeth Neil had ever seen. "Rios told me to watch out for you."

"Raul, why haven't the Japs taken this place before now?"

"We keep 'em on the run, Tomás. They think they're smart. They attack the Americans all the way from the coast on Zig Zag Pass and then they think they fall back and hold here. They make a big mistake. That's why we been one month waiting. They fall into our trap now. We kill plenty of Japs today."

"Okay, Raul. Whatever you say," Neil coughed.

This was one of the last difficult passages the American army would have to make on what was appropriately named Zig Zag Pass. The pass twisted and turned for over a hundred kilometers, and, as a main artery across the top of the Bataan peninsula, was essential to any conquering army. The pass had to be controlled, or there would be no way of advancing—or even retreating. By controlling it, the American and Filipino armies could cut off any Japanese retreat to the south and reduce the time it took to liberate Luzon. The shorter the conflict, the fewer lives lost. It was simple math. Addition and subtraction done in blood. There was no other way to do it in a war.

Raul handed Neil an old bolt-action Springfield rifle. "You might need this, Tomás."

"Thanks. How far away are the Japs, do you think?"

"Not far now. One, maybe two kilometers. They coming down the ridge. Look—" Calderas pointed to the top of the ridge. From the highest point, a flash signal was being relayed from a small mirror to Rios and the others below.

"We count thirty, maybe forty enemy soldiers. We have thirty of our men on top closing in behind the Japs. No escape. They all die soon."

"Where's Morang?" Neil voiced weakly.

"He's up there on the ridge. He and the other scouts making sure we know where all the Japs come from. They kill stragglers." He scowled as he drew a hand across his throat.

Neil had seen Morang's handiwork with a machete. The tribesman's small size disguised his strength and stealth. He couldn't criticize them, though, for feeling the way they felt, doing things the way they liked to do them. The brutal eye-for-an-eye conflict that surrounded him was deeply distasteful to him. Morally repugnant. At least in an airplane, killing was distant. Detached.

You didn't have to touch or see the face of the enemy. You could pretend the enemy had no face. Here it was completely different. It was almost as though it were a challenge to these guerrillas to see how close they could get to their enemy before killing him. Face to face. Eyeball to eyeball. An eye for an eye. And beheading had become their blood sport, a gruesome sport begun by the Japanese and now imitated gleefully by the Filipino guerrillas.

"Just got to hold on for forty-eight hours—got to make it. Do it for Caroline. Do it for little Neil. You're almost home free." He was talking to himself in whispers. He had to be strong—just awhile longer. Calderas had slid over behind some rocks next to him, his Thompson submachine gun trained on the footbridge.

Sweat poured off Neil's face. His slackened muscles strained to hold the old rifle in a firing position. His eyes narrowed at the sudden appearance of the noonday sun. He slid down behind the large boulder to wait. The sun would light up the valley for one good hour as its rays peaked over the tops of the mountains looming above the jungle canopy. The entire day in this valley was cast in shadows, with the exception of high noon. Valle de Sombros—meaning Valley of Shadows—is appropriate, Neil thought. Valley of Death. So many shadows. So many lives would be lost in them today.

"In the Presence of Mine Enemies"

1300 Hours
Rio Sombro bridge, Zig Zag Pass,
Bataan peninsula, Philippines

"Calderas," Neil whispered to his Filipino companion.

"What is it, Tomás?"

"What's the plan? Nobody has told me exactly what we're doing. What exactly are we waiting for?"

"Wait until the Japs cross the bridge. Wait till all cross. Make them think they safe. Then start shooting from both sides of river. They try to go back, we—"

Calderas's hand moved across his throat.

Before Neil could respond, the first of the Japanese soldiers darted from the cover of the far side of the bridge and set up his firing position behind an enormous log. Another two quickly followed. Neil glanced up at a rocky outcropping on the far side of the river and thought he saw an enemy machine gun set up there.

"Calderas." Neil pointed to the rocky ledge where the Japanese had set up a Nambu gun.

Calderas nodded an affirmative. He had spotted it, too.

More Japanese soldiers were coming out into the open. A group of five now began to cross the bridge. The Filipinos let them proceed. There was no noise. Even the animals in the jungle seemed to sense the danger and fell silent. Soon, another small band came out of hiding and made a dash to the footbridge. They had started inching their way across. The swaying, torrent-moistened hemp rope made footing precarious. Before long, thirty or so enemy soldiers had traversed the river and set themselves up in positions— unknowingly meters away from a much larger force of Filipino guerrillas. The guerrillas had the Japanese outflanked and surrounded. The plan had been a good one.

Raul Calderas listened for the signal. It was a call, a bird call, that one of the guerrillas would give upon the command from Rios. Neil kept his eyes on Raul and his Springfield rifle trained on the Japanese below him. He was waiting for the moment all hell would break loose. He saw Calderas nod and then looked up the ridge to read the mirror signal.

A loud, shrill sound, now issued from the far bank of the river, from behind the Japanese machine gunners' position. Then it happened. All hell broke loose. The jungle exploded in a cacophony of violence. The Japanese patrol was being slaughtered before Neil's very eyes, his own finger on the trigger.

*   *   *

Capt. Osamu Ito crawled over to the body of his radio man, Private Harada. He turned him over and began to crank the handle to the radio that still hung from his back. It had been riddled with bullets. There was no way to contact his regiment now. They were isolated. Cut off.

Bullets filled the air and kicked up the dirt around him. The small clump of boulders that barely protected him from the rage of the Filipinos' deadly fire also cut him off from his men, stripping him of his ability to command. He looked back over to the other side of the river. Scattered everywhere lay the bodies of his men. He searched for Corporal Hayashi's Nambu gun to return fire and offer cover. Nothing. It had been put out of action.

The fighting had barely begun, and it was already over. The lethal effectiveness of the ambush indicated that it had been planned for months, with accurate intelligence. He searched for a white scarf, anything he could tie to the tip of his officer sword to raise in surrender. If he could save one of his men, he would do it. Pulling out his blue bandanna from his trouser pocket, he tied it to the Samurai sword that his father had carried before him. He gazed around to search for any of his men who might still be firing. He could see no movement. Dead. All dead or wounded. He waved the makeshift flag at the same instant that a Filipino grenade landed two meters from his position.

Sergeant Ozawa had arrived at the rendezvous point, exactly as planned. From his vantage point upstream, he had watched the enemy wipe out his entire company in what felt like an instant. The Filipinos had set the perfect trap.

Using the sniper scope attached to his bolt-action rifle, Ozawa scanned the small clearings on either side of the footbridge and counted almost thirty bodies. He searched in vain for any sign of resistance from his men. There was Corporal Hayashi and his squad, sprawled out next to the Nambu machine gun, some slaughtered by exploding grenades, some by rifle fire. The gunfire in the first few seconds of the ambush had been overwhelming, like a fatal tropical rainstorm.

Ozawa was now alone. It was up to him to avenge the deaths of his comrades and to die by the code of honor he had sworn to carry out. Death before surrender. He had a perfect position, at one hundred meters. He could take out as many of the Filipino guerrillas who ventured into the open—as many as he could kill—before they spotted him.

He surveyed the scene again. He thought he could see an American among the Filipinos. He trained his gun at the rocks where the upper half of the American's torso was exposed. Ozawa was well hidden by the jungle brush. Quickly he chambered one round and took aim at the American—then he saw something move among the Japanese bodies lying prone near his target. It was a blue flag.

"Surrender!" he snorted angrily, his breath muffled. It was an officer's sword. He knew that it had to be Captain Ito. "The coward will die with honor, like his men," he growled to himself as he moved the crosshairs of the sniper scope to sight his captain. There was an explosion near the spot. Ozawa waited to see the dust settle. Ito still waved the surrender flag.

"Stand! Stand up, coward, and let me help you die with dignity." His voice was fierce as he concentrated on the target, one eye peering through the scope and the other eye closed. Every shot counted. Ito's narrow back filled the sniper scope.

The firing suddenly stopped. The silence rang in his ears. Ozawa moved quickly from the cover of the jungle canopy to a small outcropping of rocks near the river. It gave him a better field of fire. He knew he was exposing himself to certain death, but he was determined to die with honor. He had no use for weaklings. He aimed. His right index finger began to squeeze the trigger—then he hesitated. It was the American. He had come out from behind some rocks with a Filipino. Now

Ozawa had three targets. He had been given the opportunity to take three of the enemy with him. But he would have to fire quickly and with deadly accuracy.

Neil watched as the Japanese officer raised the flag again. The grenade hadn't killed him after all.

"Stop firing. Stop! Calderas, get your men to stop."

"It's a dirty Jap trick, Tomás," the Filipino sergeant called out to him.

"He's surrendering—we've killed them all, Raul. We could use an officer—a prisoner—for American Intelligence."

Calderas signaled to Rios. Rios came out from his jungle hiding place on the other side of the Rio Sombro. He signaled for his men to stop firing. The guerrillas came out of hiding from everywhere, it seemed. Rios quickly gave them instructions as he crossed the footbridge.

"Take no prisoners and leave no wounded Japs alive," he shouted. No

Japanese soldier would be shooting one of his men in the back today.

"Rios. This officer is seriously wounded. He wants to surrender. He may have valuable information for American and Filipino Intelligence. I don't want him killed." Neil stood with his back to the Japanese officer, who still sat on the ground, stunned and bleeding from the grenade explosion.

A dozen rifles were trained on the officer as Calderas ran to him and snatched the sword from his hand.

"Calderas! Stop!" Neil shouted as he moved to protect the Japanese officer.

"Get out of my way, Tomás, or I kill you, too." Calderas was in a rage. "Japs kill my brother and father. Maybe this Jap. Move, Tomás."

"That's enough killing, Raul. Enough! I'm standing here until you put the sword down. Calderas! Calderas— Rios!" Neil looked over at the Filipino lieutenant for help.

Then he turned back to the groaning enemy soldier, bent over him to examine his wounds. The Japanese officer was leaning against the small boulder that had previously offered him protection. He was trying to stand up. The crucifix that hung from Lt. Neil Thomas's neck caught the startled enemy officer's eye, and he mouthed words so softly that Neil could not hear them. Carefully Neil disarmed the officer, tossing his pistol and rifle aside, as he strained to understand what he was trying to tell him.

The enemy officer was groaning, his voice rising. Neil could make out the words now: "I Catholic. Speak English. Confession, please? I die—confession, talk—please?" The soldier's legs were bleeding badly and it appeared that the blood that soaked the sides of his uniform came from massive back wounds.

Calderas held the sword high over the officer's head.

Rios came up behind him and grabbed his arm. "No, Raul. Tomás is right this time. We take Jap. If he lives, he must talk to American Intelligence. If he don't talk, you can kill him."

The crack of rifle fire sounded from upstream; it was followed by the sickening thump of flesh being hit. The smacking sound was Raul Calderas's chest being shattered. He catapulted backward.

Another shot sounded, hitting the wounded Captain Ito in the upper shoulder, causing him to slump onto Neil. The jungle broke out in rifle fire as the Filipinos took aim at the lone Japanese sniper crouching in the open— in perfect position for target practice on the boulders nearly a hundred meters upstream.

Bullets skittered around the body of the wounded Japanese officer—now facedown at Neil's feet. The back of the officer's uniform was a pool of dark blood. Life blood. He must either leave him and get cover, or—

A strange wave of compassion ran through his body, causing him to reach for the stricken man. A single image was running through his mind. He saw, in a split second, the face of the last Japanese pilot he had killed in anger, the day Jimmy Cameron was downed over Tinian.

Ignoring the blood, ignoring his own weakness, Neil scooped the wounded man up in his arms. Holding the frail enemy soldier, he began to run through the sand to the safety of the rocky ledges that overlooked Rio Sombro. He couldn't understand where he was summoning the strength from to do it, but the adrenaline surging through him outran the bullets kicking up at his heels.

One more yard—just a couple more steps—you can make it, Neil. The sound of the Filipino's gunfire trained on the lone sniper crackled in the air around him like an angry summer storm. Neil was out of breath and out of strength, staggering with his burden.

Suddenly he felt a hot sensation fill his lower back—and he was thrown forward by the impact of sharp, piercing metal.

"God, no! Not now!" he cried out as he fell forward, the Japanese officer tumbling from his arms. Ito moaned loudly as he hit the sand hard a few feet ahead of Neil.

Neil was lying facedown. He struggled to turn over. To stand up.

Rios reached the fallen American.

He wrapped his arm over Neil's shoulder, picked him up, and carried him to the safety of the rocks. Neil, out of breath, leaned hard against the rocks, finally sliding to the ground. He could feel the blood oozing from the front of his lower stomach—and also draining down his back. "Clean through. My God—the bullet had gone clean through," he muttered.

"You make it, then. You be okay," Rios insisted. "I take care of this lousy Jap."

The sniper fire had stopped. Rios pulled out his sidearm, a .38 special. He cocked the hammer and walked over to the moaning Japanese captain. "You die now, Jap." He pointed the black six-round revolver at the head of the dying enemy officer.

Captain Ito's breathing was agonized, his half-open eyes transfixed on Neil a yard away. He was completely helpless.

"No, Rios! Please—for me. For me, Rios . . . please." Neil was coughing weakly, his breath coming in jerks and starts, his arm outstretched to plead with Rios. "He'll die anyway. Let him live now—to talk—"

The Filipino let out an angry scream and fired the bullet into the sandy ground, missing the captain's head by inches. "You die soon, Jap!"

Captain Ito opened his mouth. He said something, almost inaudible, as he lay sprawled on his side in the sand. He seemed to be looking right through Neil—through Neil's tattered shirt to where his dog tags and crucifix dangled carelessly against his wounded chest. His lips barely moved as he whispered, *"Domo . . . Domo arigato . . ."* "Thank you."

Sergeant Ozawa lay in a pool of blood. He had hit all three targets before falling mortally wounded by the return fire. He could die with honor now. Blood oozed from his mouth and he coughed as he saw a shadow appear over him. It was the shadow of a tribesman. He was helpless as he lay there, watching the small mountain man raise his machete high over his head. The blade

seemed to glisten from the sun's reflected light as the shadow descended
with it. The shadow of his death.

When the execution was over, Morang left the remains of the enemy
sniper and ran to the footbridge and to
his friend, Tomás.

Neil looked over at the dying Japanese
captain, whose mangled body two Filipino guerrillas had just carried into the
cave.

"Put him next to Tomás," ordered an
annoyed-sounding Ernesto Rios. Rios
walked over to the enemy officer,
whose bleeding had started again from
being jolted by the hurried pace. "You
talk, Jap. Maybe I save you, maybe I
don't, but you talk now."

"Water . . . please?" responded Captain Ito.

"Ramon!" Rios called to one of the
other guerrillas standing nearby. He
snapped his fingers and pointed to the
canteen against the wall.

"Here, take mine," Neil broke in. With
great effort, he reached next to him and

held the water up to the lips of the thirsty man. Ito drank greedily from the container.

"Enough," Rios growled. "You talk now! What's your name?"

"Capt. Osamu Ito, Third Regiment, Light Infantry," he said without hesitation.

"How many men in regiment? Where are the rest of them?" Rios demanded.

"Almost all dead. My company dead. Who left—fighting Americans. No more fight—please? I die. I speak. No more fight." Ito pleaded through the pain that showed all too clearly in his contorted facial expressions. His breathing was labored. His uniform was soaked through and through with his own blood.

Rios fell silent at the Japanese captain's response. His hatred and bitterness ran deep, but this man possessed something—a quiet strength and dignity that he hadn't expected. He anticipated a belligerent enemy—one he would be happy to kill.

"My name is Lt. Neil Thomas." Neil broke the silence. "Your company has been looking for me." He reached out with his trembling left hand. Ito was no more than a foot away, but the Japanese officer was too weak to respond. He just looked back at the American. A pain-filled movement of his lips was a brave attempt to fabricate a smile.

Miguel Camacho entered the cave. "I brought supplies. Got some from dead Jap. Tomás, I fix you up," the Filipino medic said as he moved next to Neil.

"Corporal Wada," Captain Ito whispered. His company medic was dead, and now the Filipino medic would benefit from the dead man's meager first-aid pack.

Neil grimaced in pain as the Filipino pulled open his shirt to inspect his wound.

"You shot all way through, Tomás," Camacho said as he kneeled in front of the American and ripped open a bag of sulfa powder to clean the wound. "Maybe it good, maybe it bad. We stop bleeding and get you to American army doctor." Camacho began to wrap the stomach and back wound in a circular wrapping that became blood-soaked as fast as he could bandage.

"Not good. You hold stomach tight and lay on back now, Tomás. Pressure stop bleeding." The medic helped Neil lie back. The repositioning caused him to let out a loud groan.

"We need doctor fast, Lieutenant Rios," Camacho told the guerrilla leader. "He die tonight from bleeding if we don't get doctor." The medic turned his attention to the Japanese officer.

Rios examined the wounded American. Neil had fought well with his men and he respected him, now more than ever—despite his weakness when it came to dispatching the captives. There wasn't the slightest hope of getting Lieutenant Thomas to an American army doctor. The Americans were still fighting their way up Zig Zag Pass. They would have to miraculously punch through stubborn Japanese resistance overnight to get there in time to save him.

"This one die soon. Not much to do here," Camacho said, as he washed the wounds and did what he could to make the Japanese captain more comfortable.

Rios, deciding to divert his attention from the dilemma that faced him in trying to save his American friend, reached for the leather satchel the Jap officer had around his neck. He opened the satchel, searched it for any military intelligence that it might contain, that might help them in their next encounter. He would gather what information he could from this Jap before he died.

"Map. Nothing else?" Rios held the contents to the weary eyes of the captured officer.

Ito's eyes grew large. He reached out toward Rios. "My crucifix."

Neil watched as Ernesto Rios dug through the satchel again. He found the crucifix and held it up to the light that was dimly glimmering from the fire in the cave.

"You're Catholic—it's true?" Neil asked, with a painful cough.

"Yes, true," returned the broken voice of the dying Ito. "A long time ago, in America, I go to Catholic college. In Los Angeles. I become Catholic there.

Please—" He reached toward Rios for the crucifix. Rios flung it at him. Ito held the crucifix to his chest as he struggled for breath.

"Catholic, Los Angeles . . . amazing," Neil coughed.

Neil felt weak, tired, in pain, but he thought he might have a chance. Looking at the Japanese officer, he knew it wouldn't be long for him now.

"You pray with me, Lieutenant Thomas? I say confession to you?" Ito's voice, weak and gravelly, was a gentle one—childlike—hardly the angry, stubborn Japanese officer Neil would have expected.

"You say what you want, Captain Ito. I listen." He studied the sweaty, ragged, and stubbly bearded man, frail, worn, and now bloodied—just like himself. He felt the brotherhood between them. They were both men, caught in the snares of war. Both Catholic. Both knew LA. Both commanded men. Both wanted to go home. The feeling caught him off guard. Moisture came to his eyes as he realized things, things the way they really were. Things the way they should be. Things . . . the way they once had been.

"First, I say words, even though you not priest?"

"Yes, whatever you want to say, Captain Ito, you say, even though I'm not a priest," Neil replied with a struggling voice, gritting his teeth in an effort to deal with the pain.

"Then, first thing. I have sinned. I want to say much—" Ito seemed to be struggling for breath. Then he coughed, spitting blood. "But I . . . I don't know how start," he managed.

"Okay, Captain Ito. We have all sinned. Let us all—" Neil sighed heavily, unable to catch a deep breath in the thickness of the cave's musty air. "Let us all," he continued, "hope we can be forgiven—for what this war has forced us to do." He looked at the ceiling of the cave, clenching his teeth as pain suddenly shot through him—a jolting sensation that made his gums throb.

"Captain Ito—you just say what comes to you." It was crazy, he thought. Two enemy soldiers, wounded, one dying and he, Lt. Neil Thomas, possibly joining him. One is confessing to the other, when sixty minutes before they were shooting at each other.

"I do not hate American or Filipino people. I sorry I kill them. I sorry I lead men to kill. I only want peace. No more war. No more hate. No more death. Forgive me, Father, for my sins." Ito was convulsing.

Rios looked at the spectacle with a mixture of cynicism and amazement. He reached for his canteen as he watched the Japanese officer struggle and walked over between him and Neil. He leaned down to Neil.

"Here, Tomás. Drink. I get you some rice to eat. You keep strength." He tilted the canteen to give his American friend a drink and then, in a mechanical way, turned around and offered the same to the dying Japanese officer.

"You're a good man, Lieutenant Rios. They make you general some . . ." Neil strained to finish the compliment that had become a special acknowledgment of their friendship.

"Yeah, sure, Tomás. You don't die.

That my first order as general." He walked back to the other side of the cave and sat down. He could wait and watch. He couldn't do more for his friend.

"Tomás! Tomás! Tomás, okay?" It was Morang. He was out of breath as he entered the cave. He appeared confused and angry as next to Neil he saw the wounded Japanese soldier. Morang turned to Rios, speaking quickly and excitedly in Tagalog. He made his familiar hand across the throat gesture as he nodded toward Ito.

"No, Morang. No kill more Japs today," Neil called out with his failing strength.

Looking like a puppy dog who didn't know how to help his stricken master, Morang turned and put his machete down.

"Morang help Tomás?" Neil asked. "Rios, please ask Morang to—aw, God, it hurts," he stammered as he clutched his stomach and looked down at the blood-soaked rags—"to reach into the hole in the wall of the cave behind me and get the ammo box." It was becoming harder to talk. Every word was a struggle. He peered over at the weakening Captain Ito, who still fingered the letter and the crucifix on his chest.

"I do it for you, Tomás," replied Rios as he got up and went over behind him and found the ammo box containing Neil's letters to Caroline. Rios set the box next to his seriously wounded American comrade and, at Neil's gesture, opened it for him.

"Thanks," Neil said with a groan. "I've got to finish something for my wife and I—" His voice failed him and he had to lay his head back for a minute to gather his strength. "I want Morang and you to take care of these things. Please get this box to the first American officer you meet, if I—if I don't make it." He looked over at Rios with a pleading face and Rios repeated the request to Morang.

"Tomás no die!" Morang insisted, and then he spoke rapidly to Rios. They carried on a conversation, with Morang growing angry and insistent about something.

Rios turned to Neil and translated. "Morang says he goes for American doctor. I tell him no way he gets through, but he says he gonna go."

"I go," Morang proclaimed as he stood and pounded his chest. He pointed to his two cousins who had appeared moments before. As he knelt down a boyishness came over the diminutive teenage fighter. He looked at Neil with tear-filled eyes and then at the Japanese in anger. He patted Neil's face like a child would pet a puppy and said, "Tomás, live. Morang go now."

"Morang, here—take—" Neil struggled as he removed the chain with his dog tags and crucifix from around his neck. It hurt to reach up with his arms. "Morang, take and give to American," Neil requested of his friend.

"Morang take. Give American," the native fighter repeated as he wiped at the moisture from his eyes that was now staining his cheeks. He put the chain around his neck and then, standing at attention, saluted stiffly. Turning to his cousins, he motioned for them to follow him and quickly left the cave.

"Good luck, my friend," Neil said as he lay back and offered a weak salute to the departing tribesmen.

Rios offered the American pilot another drink and repeated the same action for Captain Ito. He commanded something in Tagalog and the medic, Camacho, ran back in to check on Neil and the Japanese officer.

"I'm sorry, for you, Tomás. We take good care of ammo box," Rios promised, as he moved back over to the other side of the cave and took in the scene before him.

"Lieutenant Thomas," Captain Ito uttered painfully, "I need to say more."

Neil tilted his head to face Ito, a foot away. "Talk, Captain Ito. Talk as much as you can," he breathed.

"Please, take—and maybe American army send to my wife, Kyoko." He reached out a trembling hand toward Neil, wanting to give him the crucifix.

"I take it for you." Rios came back over and accepted it from the dying Japanese officer. "We put it in ammo box. It safe there."

"Thanks, Rios." Neil smiled and

added a thumbs-up signal to the Filipino. "Rios, let me hold it first."

"Sure thing, Tomás." The Filipino officer handed the crucifix to Neil, who
examined it intently and then relaxed,
holding it in his left hand. He gently
rubbed his fingers over the Christ figure with its crown of thorns. Memories
washed over him, like a gentle breeze
bearing the smell of life, fragrant life,
flowered life from home.

Captain Ito's words were barely au-
dible. "Lieutenant Thomas. I say again,
I do not hate. No more—no one—no
more, forever." The Japanese soldier
coughed violently and blood issued
from his mouth, this time more than before. More than he could spare. "Thomas, I die. Psalms . . . you pray with
me?" Ito's mouth filling with blood
caused him to gurgle as he spoke.

"Yes, sir, Captain," Neil replied, in an
exhausted, pain-racked voice. He
knew what the captain wanted. The
Twenty-third Psalm. Neil had memo-
rized the short verses in catechism
classes as a child, had repeated them
often before departing on dangerous

missions. There was a comfort in them. He understood why the Japanese officer wanted to hear the words, to pray the words. Neil began with great effort as he enunciated each word deliberately, taking breaths as he went.

" *'The Lord . . . is my shepherd . . .'* " he began. *" 'I shall not want. He maketh me to lie down . . . in green pastures . . . he leadeth me beside the still waters. He restoreth my soul . . .' "*

Neil's chest heaved as he sought air to continue. He stopped as a sharp, stabbing pain shot through his abdomen, causing him to grimace. He forced air through his teeth, with his jaw clenched tight in an effort to hold off the pain. He took in another deep breath and started again.

" *'He leadeth me . . . in the paths of righteousness for his name's sake. Yea, though I walk through the valley of the shadow . . .'* " Neil paused. A chill swept through him as he realized that they lay in the valley named by the verse, both of them dying from their wounds. He looked over at the deathly still Captain Ito. Tears suddenly coursed down his face. He gazed into the ceiling of the cave seeking the rest of the familiar words.

" 'Yea, though I walk . . . through the valley . . . of the shadow . . . of death . . . I will fear no evil.' "

The Japanese soldier strained to speak as he listened, his lips moving with every word Neil prayed. More blood spilled from his mouth as he weakly whispered the prayer in harmony with the American.

" 'For thou art with me . . . thy rod and thy staff . . . they comfort me . . . Thou preparest a table before me . . . in the presence of mine enemies . . .' "

Neil reached to touch the hand of the dying man, to let him know—to let him know he was not alone in death. He had never touched his enemy before. He took another breath, fighting the exhaustion and the pain. His emotions had surfaced. He struggled to finish.

" 'In the presence of mine enemies . . . Thou anointest my head with oil . . . my cup runneth over.' "

He turned his head and looked again at Captain Ito. The officer's breathing had stopped. His mouth still drained blood and his eyes were fixed open as he lay in death's stillness.

" 'Surely goodness and mercy shall follow me . . . all the days of my life: and I will dwell . . . in the house of the Lord . . . for ever.' "

Susan put the pages down gently, almost reverently. She was in awe of the man who fought to return home to his family so many years ago.

She looked at the roses Neil had sent to her. *Could he be anything like his father?* she wondered as she turned out the light, anxious for the night to become day and to see him once again.

The Return Home

Saturday, January 31, 1998
Pasadena, California

I'd spent the better part of Saturday morning packing and cleaning my mother's house, checking my watch every few minutes, excited and nervous about seeing Susan again. I was surprised at how I was feeling this morning, about the packing. Once I made a decision, generally, I didn't look back. I had decided to let this house go its way, to move in another direction. Now I was having doubts, although I wasn't yet ready to face them and ask myself what they meant. I kept myself distracted by rearranging the old photos for the interview, placing a few on the mantel next to my mother's crystal clock. I planned to take down my father's old plaque from over the entry door, the quote from the Bible that he'd hung with so much love, but eventually decided to leave it up for now. I was hoping Susan would notice; its words had been a guiding principle in my life.

Satisfied that the room was ready, I glanced at my watch again. The morning had crawled, but it was finally about time for her to arrive.

I hadn't seen her since we walked the mall in Washington, D.C., ten days before. So much had happened in such a short time, and I didn't know what to make of my feelings for her. I had lost sleep the last few days, allowing myself to picture a new life with her. I wanted her to know I understood the emptiness she felt; but every time I'd started to speak, my mind would return to Diane, making me feel as if I were somehow betraying her.

Now, peering out the window, looking for a sign of Susan's car, my thoughts turned to my wife again. Our love had been special, more than most people find in a lifetime, but she was gone now, and I had to go on. She'd want me to be happy again, to love again—wouldn't she? I thought back to our final day together.

January 1995
Los Angeles, California

Was it the rain that moistened my face and formed the salty droplets of life that caused this taste on my lips? Or was it the tears that swept from my eyes in torrents, drowning my joys, filling my cup with such sorrow?

Standing at Diane's grave had been as bittersweet as the heaven-sent rain mixing with my own fountain of emotion.

I couldn't help it. The crowds were gone, the service ended. The kids, Rachel and Eric, were waiting in the limousine. I needed to thank her, thank God, be grateful privately for the twenty-seven wonderful years that I'd lived with the woman who had been such a light in my life.

Diane. My mind now replayed the memory of our final moment together. Breast cancer had eaten away at her bubbling enthusiasm for a year. It had drained her until death's angel closed her eyes, just a few nights before, as I held her in my arms.

"It's okay, sweetheart. You can go now. I love you so much," I had whispered. "I will always love you, Diane. It's okay. Wait for me, honey. I promise I'll find you again." I had cried softly as I watched her struggle for her last breaths.

Nothing had prepared me for this. I had seen men die in Vietnam—friends—but not this. I felt as if a part of me were dying. Half of life leaving me. I gained a new respect for life, the fleetingness of it all, and for the love—the endurance one must have to hold on to it.

Bending over her bed, I laid my head against her chest to hear the last rhythms of life as her body relaxed at my offer to let go. I embraced her, wrapping my strong arms around her frail body. She hadn't spoken for days, and I longed to hear a word from her lips, any words, one final time. My love story was ending, just as my mother's had the year before.

I convinced myself that I was hearing her voice in my mind, repeating those three sacred words that I longed to hear. I raised my head, seeking the life in her eyes—one final time. I stroked her forehead, kissed her cheeks.

A feeling of electricity shot through me as her eyes suddenly flew open. I searched her face, wondering if this was life's final reflex. But when her eyes turned toward mine, they were wet with tears—with life. I smothered her with kisses, cradling her head. Her breathing eased, and she whispered the precious words I was hoping to hear. Our life together was ending with a sweetness I could never have expected.

Then her eyes closed. A solitary tear touched my lips as I kissed her. As I felt her body relax next to mine, I repeated the words tenderly, "I love you. I will always love you, Diane."

When the doorbell rang, I was still lost in thought, checking the living room one last time.

Susan was glowing, even more beautiful than I'd remembered. I greeted her with a warm smile, then proudly ushered her into the living room, showing her what I'd done. She smiled in appreciation and praised my handiwork, her eyes taking in the house, the softness of her words seeming to mirror the mood she had found me in. She reached down and opened her attaché case. She pulled out a videotape.

"Glad there's still a TV and VCR here," she said. "Thought you might like to see a finished copy of Colonel Jackson's interview, see what it looks like now that our film editors have worked their magic on it."

"I'd love that," I replied, "but let's go out for a while first, have a cup of coffee, and I'll show you the sights. I've been here too long this morning," I finished, laughing. "This packing is getting to me."

"Sounds great," she said. "All right if I leave my stuff here?" gesturing toward her case.

"Sure! How 'bout we watch the tape together?" I asked.

"I'd like that," she responded sweetly.

We spent the rest of the afternoon driving around Pasadena, ending up at Alameda and Olvera Streets in downtown LA. I slowed the car as we passed by Union Station—they'd be shooting the train station footage late Monday evening, two days from now, and Susan wanted to get a sense of the setting. But we'd lost track of time, absorbed in conversation as we drove around town, and we were both anxious to get back and watch the interview before she returned to her hotel for the evening.

I opened my mouth before I knew what I was saying. An opportunity had presented itself, and I asked her if she'd like to have an early dinner with me at La Golondrina restaurant before the taping Monday, saying it would be a great way to experience the magic of that part of the story before the interview on Tuesday afternoon.

Much to my relief, she accepted, grinning—as if I'd read her mind. We drove back to the house then, making ourselves comfortable in front of the television. I never asked if she'd finished the story—it didn't matter somehow. Something was changing in her, as if she had blossomed, and I didn't want to break the spell. Once again, we listened to Colonel Jackson tell his story. I felt content—it had been too long since I'd felt the way I was feeling now. I had almost forgotten how emotions of peace felt.

October 20, 1993
Zig Zag Pass, Bataan peninsula,
Philippines

"Where are we, Miguel?" asked retired army colonel David Jackson.

"We are close to the village now. Two, maybe three kilometers. Just down road before the pass start up again. Rio Sombro is on other side of ridge." The old ex-Filipino army sergeant pointed west toward the jungle village.

"Are you sure the tribal guerrilla fighter you spoke of is still living?" asked Jackson.

"To be sure, I cannot say. We'll know in a couple of minutes, though."

David Jackson studied the jungle landscape around him as he rode in the passenger seat of the old Willys Army Jeep. It reminded him of Vietnam and he could visualize the scenes of guerrillas ambushing the Japanese occupiers in a war now forty-eight years in the past.

"I saw him last year for the first time in forty-eight years," Miguel said, breaking the silence. "He came to the army clinic set up in the village. I was supervisor, before I retired. He looked healthy enough. Never can tell though. We World War II guys are getting old." Miguel Camacho grinned as he drove the old jeep over the bumpy dirt road section of Zig Zag Pass.

"There—there over on your right, above the tree line. See the smoke? Two hundred meters. That's where we find Morang."

Jackson anxiously anticipated talking to the old guerrilla fighter. He had served as an infantry officer from 1962 until retirement in 1992. He had seen action as a young rifle company commander in Vietnam. He had earned the Bronze Star and two Purple Hearts. He rose through the ranks through two tours of duty, ending in 1970 with the rank of major. Commanding a battalion in 1969, with the First Cavalry Division, he had a special appreciation for guerrilla fighters—in fact, he had been on the receiving end of their special tactics. The Japanese had been subjected to the same in the Philippines at the end of World War II.

For the remainder of his military career Jackson had served first in the Pentagon and then as an instructor at West Point. As an analyst in the Pentagon he had been instrumental in forming policies and procedures for the all-new "volunteer" army. At West Point he taught history and was able to offer special perspectives to instruction in "nonconventional" warfare and military campaigns. He had been intrigued at how, so often during World War II, it was small ambushes and small company-sized campaigns that made the difference in the outcome of key major battles. While the history books pointed out the successes of the larger battles, information or credit was seldom given to the down and dirty skirmishes of individual squads, platoons, or companies of soldiers that made all the difference. In timing, saving lives, securing operations zones, setting up communications, and destroying enemy weapons and strongholds, these small groups of guerrillas and behind-the-lines commandos gave the larger invasion forces an important edge. Often forgotten, the relentless guerrilla attacks, time after time, broke the enemy's ability to resist the U.S. and Allied Armies' assaults.

Now, as a retired U.S. Army colonel, Jackson was working for the Smithsonian Institute in Washington, D.C. His natural interest in the combat roles of Americans engaged in guerrilla warfare blended well with his first assignment, which was to study small guerrilla engagements that had helped shape the tide of victory in the Philippines during World War II. Perhaps nowhere like the Philippines were there more engagements that affected the successful outcome of the returning American forces under Gen. Douglas MacArthur in 1944.

One such engagement was a little-known battle fought over a section of road on the Zig Zag Pass that ran through the top of the Bataan peninsula. The battle for the Rio Sombro bridge was a costly one for the Japanese. The American army's Sixth Corps had landed on the west coast of Bataan in early January 1944 to secure the road and cut off retreating Japanese army units from the northern Luzon regions. It was a dirty job that had U.S. infantry units slugging it out for two months with a tenacious foe. The Japanese made them pay for every kilometer of the pass. The Filipinos, attacking from the rear, had given the American forces a much-needed advantage, one that was instrumental in saving time and the lives of many soldiers. The bridge at Rio Sombro was located in a narrow valley and pass that would allow the Japanese a strategic advantage over the Americans, if they held onto it. The Filipinos came to the rescue, and it was the battle of Rio Sombro that was the focus of Col. David Jackson's current studies.

"We almost there, Colonel," Miguel Camacho said, as the Jeep rounded a bend. "See? There. Cayan. Much bigger now. Then it was just a sleepy village with tribal natives, some Filipinos. We ask at the first house. Morang is well-respected leader of tribal clan. His father was leader, but killed by Japs. Everybody knows him. They take us to him."

The old, one-legged mountain villager was no more than four and one half feet tall. Bent with age, he ambled out of his hut with the help of his home-made crutch. He wore old, tattered khaki shorts and a shirt resembling a World War II Filipino scout uniform, frayed and faded to a dull gray color. He looked at the tall retired American first and then at Miguel Camacho, and with the aid of his crutch, stiffened to a straight attention position, offering a military salute. Tears came freely to his eyes as Miguel came forward and embraced the aging World War II guerrilla fighter.

"Morang, I want to introduce you to Col. David Jackson from the U.S. Army," he said in Tagalog. "Colonel Jackson, this is the guerrilla fighter scout, Morang. He was good guerrilla fighter."

"I honored. I love America. I welcome American." Morang gestured for the two men to enter his small one-room hut, motioning for them to be seated on floor mats.

"I wait long. Camacho—you give Tomás," Morang said, as he took a chain off from around his neck and handed to the surprised Miguel a set of old American serviceman dog tags and a crucifix. Morang pointed to the tall American. "You give now. Tomás say, you give American." He gestured with his hand anxiously as the ex-Filipino army medic handed the chain and the dog tags to David Jackson.

Miguel's surprise quickly turned into questions as he queried the old tribesman about how he had gotten the dog tags and crucifix and what he was talking about. Miguel had attended to the wounds of the American lieutenant in his final hours and knew of Morang's attempt to get through to American lines to bring medical help for Tomás. He now wanted to know the rest of the story. Until seeing him the year before, in 1992, he thought Morang had been killed. He listened as the excited old guerrilla fighter's story unfolded. A rapid exchange of words occurred in the conversation in Tagalog that bridged a nearly five-minute time span. Jackson was anxious to know what was being said. Miguel Camacho finally stopped and turned to him to relate it.

"I explained to Morang why we visiting. That you study the war. Then he tells me about our American fighter friend, Tomás. I treated his wounds at the Battle of Rio Sombro."

Colonel Jackson examined the name on the dog tags. "Lt. Neil Thomas, USN, the serial number and religion—Catholic," he stated out loud. "Where did he get these?"

"He says Tomás—that what we call him—Tomás told him to give them to first American officer he sees. You first American officer he sees since war."

"Wait—you mean he has had these dog tags for almost fifty years?"

"Yes," the Filipino Miguel Camacho shrugged.

"Then, this Lt. Neil Thomas was never known to have served with you until now?" Jackson was clearly excited at the discovery. An American had fought with these guerrillas, an unknown American. He gazed at Camacho and then over at Morang, who sat there proud and erect, his back straight, as he sensed he had at last fulfilled his American friend Tomás's final wish.

"Well, I think Americans know. He was a pilot. Japs shoot him down. Morang find him and bring him to us. He with us two, maybe three months. Good fighter. He was waiting for American army. He almost make it, then the Battle of Rio Sombro. But I think American leaders know." Until now, Camacho had been certain that Tomás was accounted for by the Americans.

Morang broke in, "I take American to box."

"Box? What box? What's he talking about, Miguel?" asked Jackson. His voice could not contain his excitement.

Miguel Camacho questioned Morang further and all the while the animated tribesman responded with quick hand motions, finally drawing one hand across his throat to indicate death.

"He says Tomás leave many things in ammo box. Morang told to take care of—give to army officer. They still in cave near Rio Sombro bridge, maybe twenty kilometers over hill."

"Let's go!" Jackson was a man on a mission. In search of history, history lost in the shadows for fifty years.

The old Jeep wound its way up the steep mountain grade and came to a halt at the crest. The three men got out.

"There. Below. There is Rio Sombro. Valle de Sombros. River is hard to see. It is more like a small stream until the rains hit. Then it overflows and washes out the bridge. You can see it if you follow the tree line. See?" Miguel Camacho pointed to the area he wanted Jackson to look at. David Jackson peered through his binoculars. The footbridge. The villagers still keep it in repair.

"There, on the far side, is where we lost Raul Calderas to a sniper. Then Tomás hit. Crazy sniper," Camacho said, shaking his head. "Sniper shot Jap officer who was surrendering. But Morang, here—he finished off the Jap sniper." Camacho thumped Morang on the back and then explained to him in Tagalog what he had just told Colonel Jackson.

Jackson listened to their exchange with half his attention. He was still intently searching the valley below through the binoculars.

"Kill all Japs," the aging tribesman said proudly.

Jackson finally spoke up. "The valley is appropriately named. Valley of the Shadows. The surrounding hills, the dense jungle foliage, and the darkness all combine to make it excellent guerrilla territory. It's hard to make out anything, even at midday."

Zig Zag Pass traversed the mountains in a winding snakelike pattern for hundreds of kilometers. No doubt it had earned its name from the Americans who had won the Philippines from the

Spanish in the Spanish-American War of 1898. It was slow going in the best vehicles. It made an ideal target for the Japanese as they defended Luzon against the advancing American army in January and February 1945. If the Japanese had captured the valley and the bridge over the Rio Sombro, they could have conceivably held the Americans at bay for weeks. It would have cost hundreds of casualties, Jackson estimated in silent reverie.

"Where exactly is this cave we're looking for?" Jackson asked Miguel.

"It's over on top of ridge, above road on other side of river. See? Look at cliff above bridge." Miguel pointed. The ledges were draped with thick, hanging vegetation, obscuring the cave opening.

"We go." Morang turned to get into the Jeep ahead of Miguel and David Jackson.

"Okay. Let's roll, Miguel." Jackson climbed into the right passenger seat. Miguel started up the engine and turned back onto the road that led to the valley's jungle floor below.

Arriving at the bridge, Miguel stopped the Jeep. All three men got out. "Here we ambush Japs. From both sides of river. Our men were here, over there, there." He pointed to strategic positions that surrounded them. "Japs had no chance. Good thing we here first," Miguel finished.

"I agree. This terrain provides excellent defensive positions. Good field of fire from almost any direction. It was a brilliant trap." Jackson looked around him at the high looming mountains, at the jungle canopy, and at the road called Zig Zag Pass. A few men with grenades, mortars, and small arms could hold up a column of tanks and armored personnel carriers for weeks. The narrow gap would be a death trap if a well-prepared enemy commanded the terrain. He reasoned that it was indeed a good thing the Filipinos held this ground for the advancing American army during the week of February 14, 1945.

"We drive across bridge and walk up to cave," Miguel announced.

"I'll walk across. You go ahead. I

want to get a feel for this place," Jackson answered.

The shadows from the surrounding ridges created an ominousness that filled the atmosphere like a dark aura. It was tangible, almost as though you could taste it, smell it. Jackson felt he could breathe the danger. Old feelings stirred—feelings he thought were long since buried—dark, oppressing feelings: Vietnam, ambushes, instant death, the sounds of jungle animals followed by sudden quiet, followed by explosions of violence—it all came back to him now. He knew what the Filipinos must have done to the Japanese company they slaughtered there.

"You like our little trap?" Miguel asked as David Jackson crossed the narrow river to the other side where he had been waiting.

"Not much hope of surviving an ambush here, unless you take prisoners," responded Jackson.

"We take only one prisoner. Jap captain. Tomás say let him live. But he died anyway."

"You took a prisoner? Where? Did

you speak to him? What did he say?" Jackson eagerly grilled Miguel for information, pulling out his notebook.

"Wait, wait. One thing at a time. Yes. We took captain. Named Ito. Up to cave. He speak very little, really. He tell us all his men wiped out. His regiment all gone; then he talk about praying. Told Tomás something and they pray together, I think. He said he was Catholic, but I don't know. He lived a little time. I tried to patch him up, but damn sniper put a bullet in his chest so bad, he lose too much blood. Look right over there." Miguel pointed to some boulders near the trail leading to the cave.

"Tomás, he was behind boulders during ambush. He fight good. This Jap captain almost killed by grenade, but still alive and tries to surrender with blue flag. Sgt. Raul Calderas, he thinks it a Jap trick and takes sword from injured captain to kill him. Then Tomás, he comes over and stops Raul. Before you know it, Jap captain shot in back by his own man. Damn Jap sniper then kills my friend Raul Calderas, right where you stand. Then Tomás, he was standing here, he picks up Jap captain in his arms and starts to run back to these boulders for protection. I don't know what he was thinking. Jap die anyway.

"So sniper shoots one more time. We all shooting at sniper now. He was upstream, one hundred meters maybe. Anyway, he hits Tomás, clean through lower back. Bad wound because Tomás bleeds so much. Too bad. We all like Tomás so much. One damn good American fighter. Well, then we shoot sniper and Morang finish him off with machete. We take Jap and Tomás to cave." Miguel looked around as if the scene, the faces, and the time was 1945 again.

"Did the Japanese captain live long? How about Thomas?" Jackson asked.

"Come, Camacho, Jackson. Come, we go now." Morang waved for them to follow him up the trail. The little man with one leg used his crutch with expert skill as he pulled himself up the steep grade. The narrow trail was overgrown, but it appeared that it was still used occasionally nevertheless. Jackson and

Camacho struggled to keep up with the aging tribesman, Morang.

"He's one tough old guerrilla fighter, Colonel Jackson," Camacho said, panting heavily. "He said earlier at his hut that he comes three, maybe four times every year, to clean cave, check on box, and cut weeds down at To-más's grave. I was surprised. I thought Tomás was buried in American ceme-tery. I thought his box went to Ameri-can army."

Jackson stopped in the middle of the trail. "You mean to tell me he knows where the remains of Lieutenant Thomas are?" Jackson was staring at Miguel incredulously. He had just stumbled onto the remains of a missing World War II hero. It didn't happen. It was not an everyday, every year—not even an every decade—event. It was a miracle. He wondered what else he would find. What the ammo box would reveal. He shook his head, caught his breath, and continued to follow after Morang, who had disappeared ahead of them.

After ten hard minutes of climbing,

they found themselves at the entrance to a cave, well-concealed by natural jungle foliage. It was obvious that Morang had perfected the camouflage over the years by adding palm fronds and old tree branches, which he pulled away expertly. He then took out from his khaki trouser pocket a small ivory-handled pocketknife and cut away the newly tangled vines. Spreading the philodendrons aside, he motioned for Jackson and Camacho to enter.

"Nice pocketknife," Jackson said to Morang as the diminutive man carefully folded the blade and put it back into his trousers. "Had one just like it when I was a kid."

"Tomás give to Morang. Morang love Tomás. Good American," answered the old mountain villager.

David Jackson mused at the devotion of the aged tribesman fighter for the American his two traveling companions called Tomás. He watched as Morang crouched down and kindled a small fire with dry brush and wood shavings he evidently kept in supply. After a minute the fire leaped and blazed and lit the cliffside room well enough to see the size and shape of the cavern.

The height of the cave made six-foot-tall Jackson bend down as he stood there. The other two men could stand perfectly erect, avoiding the jagged cave ceiling.

"Forty-eight years," reminisced Miguel aloud. "Forty-eight years ago since I have not seen this place. We leave next day after Battle at Rio Sombro. Americans come. We take fight to Manila." Miguel Camacho's eyes darted around the small room as he took in a deep breath. It was as if he were observing a sacred moment of ceremonial devotion. Jackson kept silent as the two aging warriors seemed to speak with thoughts of a time long since passed.

Morang began to dig behind a small boulder and finally pulled an old green metal ammunition box out of its hiding place. It was like the consecration of the mass, a moment of high reverence, for the devout old tribesman. He grasped the box as if it were the host

itself, a sacred treasure he was entrusted to care for. He walked over to
the retired American army officer and
held the box with outstretched hands
toward him.

"Tomás, say—give American. You
take." There was a hint of tears as Morang nodded to the American, who acknowledged the importance of the
moment by looking directly into the
tribesman's eyes. "Now Morang true.
Now word good. I do for Tomás." Morang then said something in Tagalog to
Camacho. The exchange was brief, but
the tone implied to Jackson that Morang was insisting on something.

"Morang says he tell you why it take
so long to give to American officer. He
wants to say why, before you open
box. He wants to know he is doing the
right thing and that you will take care
of Tomás's box."

Jackson was astounded. Here the little man, so protective, had kept secrets
to the life and death of an American
serviceman locked up for almost fifty
years. In keeping his word, he had also
kept the survivors of the lieutenant in

the dark for all of those years. But the little man possessed his own kind of honor, and Jackson respected that.

"Tell Morang we sit and listen. Tell him he should tell me his story and anything else he would like to say. Tell him he has done very good for Tomás and that I would like to see where Tomás is buried. Tell him Tomás should go home to America with his box. It is a good thing that he did, and the family and friends of Tomás will be very happy. Tell him that I go back to America and tell a good story to the American people about Filipino fighters. Tell him that, please, Miguel."

Miguel Camacho began to translate to Morang, who nodded his approval. Morang neared the American and reached out his hand again. Jackson gave him a warm handshake and pat on the shoulder and gestured for him to sit with him on the floor of the cave.

Morang began to tell Camacho what had happened to him after he left Tomás in the cave. The session lasted about one half hour. Miguel told him

what he saw in the final hour of Tomás's life.

"Like Morang says, he try to go to get
American doctor for Tomás. Our Filipino company leader, Ernesto Rios,
tells him no way. But he goes anyway.
The Japs retreat between us and advancing Americans. Lots of fighting on
Zig Zag Pass. Japs running around,
trying to set up ambush for Americans.
Americans shooting at everything that
moves in front of them. Morang and a
cousin get through Jap lines and almost to Americans when Americans
start shooting. Morang, confused, gets
shot in legs. Cousin shot in hand and
arm. They lie there and Americans
come close to finish them off. American
soldier sees that it's Filipino he shoots.
They hurry and get Morang and cousin
to medics. Morang shot up pretty bad.
He tries to tell them about Tomás, but
nobody listens. Then they put him out.
He wakes up with one leg gone.

"He knows Tomás dead by then.
He's plenty mad. He tries to tell Filipino

translator about Tomás. They give him the brush off. They tell him not to worry. He can't find Tomás's dog tags and crucifix. He explains to Filipino nurse. The nurse brings American doctor, who has dog tags, and starts to ask him questions. He thinks that maybe they finally help. Morang tells the American that he takes them to the cave. They say yes, but do nothing. He watches American doctor go and hang up dog tags on hook by nursing room. Finally he tells his cousin to get him out of hospital and take him home. He goes at night. He takes dog tags from hook. He goes to Rio Sombro. Nobody there. He goes to find Tomás. Sees two fresh graves outside cave. He knows Jap and Tomás not make it. Morang is angry with Americans and then decides to tell American officer only. He tries many times, but war going fast. Nobody listens. So he goes home. He tries many times after war ends, but always something bad happens. He says to God that when right American comes, he gives him Tomás's things and keeps word. You the right American."

"I think I understand. Tell him that he did the right thing," Jackson added. Miguel interpreted the American's words to Morang, who, seemingly satisfied, relaxed.

"Miguel, ask him if he will show us the graves," Jackson said. As if Morang understood, the little man was up and, leaning on his crutch, was heading for the cave opening, motioning for them to follow.

"I think he understands English pretty good," smiled Camacho as they exited behind Morang.

They walked up the hill to a small clearing not far from the cave entrance. It became apparent to Jackson that someone kept the area clear from trees and jungle growth. The elephant grass grew over two humplike elevations in the small, flat jungle clearing. At closer inspection, a small wooden cross became visible at the head of each mound, with stones piled neatly around it, clearly marking the location of the American and Japanese graves.

The three men stood there solemnly. Miguel knelt down in front of one of the graves, overcome with emotion. He hadn't expected to feel the stirrings come out. He thought the Americans had found the place long ago. He had just assumed that Lieutenant Tomás's death was known to them, and that they had come back for the body and buried him in the American cemetery at Clark Field or in Manila. The Filipinos who fought with them loved them because the Americans died with them for their freedom. Ernesto Rios was going to tell the Americans, but then was killed two days later. Miguel made the sign of the cross and got up from his knees. Wiping away the tears, he turned to Jackson.

"I'm sorry. I buried Tomás and the Japanese captain myself." Just then a thunderhead appeared and rain began to pour out of the sky. "Come into the cave. I tell you about Lieutenant Tomás and then you open box. Come." Miguel started for the cave. Morang paused in front of the grave, and then, standing as stiffly erect as his crippled body would allow, saluted.

The three men came back together inside the cave as the thunder rolled and the rain plunged in torrents.

"I tell you the story of a good man," Miguel began as they sat around the small fire.

February 14, 1945
Zig Zag Pass, Bataan peninsula,
Philippines

Neil held his hand to his stomach wound. Miguel had just taken Ito's body out for burial. Morang had been gone for a few hours. Neil could hear the distant crack of rifle and artillery fire. He knew that the Americans were advancing. If he just held on through the night. But he was getting weaker by the minute, or maybe just tired. He wanted to sleep. He was sick with dysentery and malaria, and his body was thinner than it had been in his entire adult life. The wound was bad. The blood—he couldn't stop it. Sleep—he had to fight it. "Rios," he called out weakly.

Rios had fallen asleep. He rubbed his eyes and answered, "Yeah—Tomás, what is it?"

"Can you help me? I don't . . . want to fall asleep." Sleep would be giving up. Sleep would be death. Neil fought for breath. It was an effort for him just to speak. "Could you—could you prop me up against the wall? Maybe I can stay awake. I'd like to write something to my wife." Neil strained through his teeth to get his message out. He'd never had to endure the kind of pain and torment he was going through now.

Ernesto Rios came over to him and gently raised him up as he reached underneath the American to scoop him into his arms. Rios was shocked at the bony frame of his American comrade. The shrinking of this man had happened so subtly. He had forgotten what the strong healthy-looking lieutenant he had met only three months before had even looked like.

Neil groaned at the pain of being

moved. "Why now?" he whispered. "Thanks. Thanks, Ernesto." He reached into the open ammo box next to him. He fumbled, trying to find the letter he had written the day before—to his infant son.

"Here, let me help you, Tomás." Rios reached for the letter sitting on top.

"Rios," Neil groaned. "In my pocket. Picture . . . card for my wife . . ." The pain was general all over the agonized face of his American friend as Rios found the small black-and-white picture, soiled from so much handling by his American friend, framed inside a white trellis constructed from C-ration cardboard.

"Here, Tomás." He laid the Valentine on the lieutenant's lap, along with the letter and photo where he could easily hold it.

"Thank you, Rios. You're a good man. They make . . . you . . ." But the struggle to talk was too much for Neil. He was gasping for air in the stale cave, his breaths more and more ragged and erratic.

"Yeah, sure. I know. They make me

general someday. You rest, Tomás. Americans be here soon. You see."

Neil looked down at the picture on his lap. He squinted as he labored to focus. Miguel Camacho, the medic, had returned to the cave and could see his struggle. He put more wood on the fire so that Neil could see better.

"Thanks, Miguel. It's so cold—I'm freezing. You guys cold?"

The two Filipinos looked at Neil and shook their heads sadly. It was over 100 degrees Fahrenheit in the cave. Their unsteady glances confirmed the knowledge that he was slipping away, and fast.

Miguel brought another blanket to cover Neil's shivering body. He knew that the loss of so much blood had caused the American's temperature to drop dangerously low.

"Just the malaria kicking in again. Right, Miguel?" Neil's teeth were chattering as he tried to smile at the Filipino wrapping the blanket around him.

"That was real nice prayer you say for Jap," Miguel answered, avoiding his question about malaria.

"You think so?" Neil shivered a response.

"Yeah, you make a good priest." Miguel helped the lieutenant bring his picture and card up where he could see them. Two of the remaining rose petals fell onto the ground.

"Miguel, my eyes are not so good right now. I want to read the letter I wrote to my son." He coughed and swallowed hard as he continued. "I wrote it yesterday. You read English?"

"Yeah, sure. Not too fast, but I learn when I was young."

"Read my letter back to me. I want to make sure it's all there." Neil's eyes fought to focus as he struggled with one hand to hold his wound and the other to hold the picture framed within the Valentine. He laid the picture on his lap where he could see it. The Japanese officer's crucifix hung from his neck. His fingers touched the crown on the head of the small Christ figure.

"Yeah, sure, Tomás. I read slowly." Camacho took the letter out of the envelope.

Rios sat across the cavernlike room

and watched glumly. He knew that it was the end for his American friend. *If only he'd left the Jap alone*, he thought. He was mad about it. All he could do now was watch and wait.

Miguel Camacho, in halting words, slowly began to read:

February 13, 1945, Philippines

Dear Son,

I wanted to write you this letter even though I know that you are not old enough now to understand. I may not be able to come home after this war. Your mother will tell you all about me, about this awful world war and what happened to me—why I couldn't come home. I want you to know that, with all my heart, I do want to come home. I want to come home to Marengo Avenue and play with you under the giant magnolia, be with you, take you to school, to baseball games . . . I want to be your dad.

Sometimes bad things happen to good people. It's just part of life, and though it seems unfair, it's really not.

I've learned that there are things more important than life . . . although I never thought I would. Father O'Donnell, at Saint Andrew's on Raymond Street, he will tell you what I mean if this letter doesn't make sense.

I've found some truths I want you to know about. I've written down many things in the letters in the ammo box where I store them, but especially in this one, my last, I want to explain some deep feelings of mine. I want to speak to you somehow, and right now this is the best way.

I've found the meaning of love while I've been at war. Now that I've known your mother, now that I've experienced combat and death in the air, at sea, and now on the ground in the Zambales of the Philippines, I think I know the meaning of the most important four-letter word in our language. Love.

Here's the secret: Love is found when you don't have to give it. It is the emotion of generosity and kindness that is compelled by no one. It is performed on the battlefield, in our daily tasks, in the marketplace, the factories, at school, in the offices, and in the halls and corridors of government. . . . But only when one truly gives of himself and without compulsion. No force, no law, no coercion can cause one to love. . . . It cannot be arranged. It is freely chosen and freely given and not given only when life flows along like a song.

True love is like a metal tested in a fire. Fires of adversity surround us daily. Are we to love when it is merely convenient? Like gold or silver, which very hot fires must heat to purge them of impurities, love must be thrust into the fire from time to time to make it purer, stronger and more resilient. And in the same way, love shines its brightest right out of the flames.

The beauty of the rose and its fragrance? There's another example of the quality that I'm trying to explain to you. The fragrance is found in the blossoms of the rose. The blossoms are found after the rosebud opens. Notice the stem on the rose bush. Notice that the bud doesn't even open until the thorns, those prickly things that can stick you and cause you to bleed, are fully formed. It's as if the rose bush is saying, "No! You can't have my beautiful flowers and the sweet smell of their petals. If you try to take one, I'll hurt you!" Is it worth risking the thorns to have the rose? It's where the blossoms dwell. Above the thorns, you will find the prize.

So it is with life. The thorns, the prickly problems of life, cause us to strive to rise above them and then, as we do, we learn. We learn to exercise true compassion, true kindness—or the thorns, if we let them, cause us to brood, to mourn over our trials. Then we plant the seeds of bitterness, hate, and ruin—weeds. We may reach up for the rose or down to the weeds . . . the weeds in life that tangle us, strangle us, and cause us to lose hope.

The great discovery I have made is that we are all free. All of us experience disappointment—the thorns in life— rich, poor, male, female, it doesn't matter. And we may either praise God for the opportunity to reach for the prize or curse him for our fate. I've heard God's name used in a variety of ways in this war. Some men praise him and others blame him, but when a man is under the gun, his life is on the line, all believe in him.

Father O'Donnell once told me something very important before I left for the war. He quoted a Scripture from the Old Testament. In Proverbs chapter four verse twenty-three you will read:

"Keep thy heart with all diligence; for out of it are the issues of life."

I didn't know what he meant then, but I do now. It has to do with knowing what really matters in life, what matters most. Then as you do know what things really matter to you, you possess the key to the door of happiness and satisfaction.

The choice will be yours, Son. Never doubt that I love you. And when you face the fires, when you feel the stabbing pain of the thorns, someone will be watching, and hoping that you choose to reach for the rose—the symbol of love.

Choose love, my son. Choose to give generously and then live with the

*consequences. I want you to be a good
man. Love your mother. Treat others
like you would have them treat you.
You are always in my thoughts. I love
you . . . very, very much!*

*Forever your loving father,
Lieutenant Neil Thomas, Sr., USN*

"Tomás! Tomás! . . . you listen?" Miguel prodded the lieutenant as he laid
the letter down next to the picture. He
shook Neil gently by the shoulder.

"Huh? . . . Oh, yeah, I uh . . . just
closed my eyes to listen. It's good, isn't
it, Miguel?" Neil started to rub the crucifix again as if he would hold on to life
by doing it. He didn't seem to struggle
so much for words now. His voice was
faint and weak, but the struggle was
gone. The voice of Miguel reading,
even with the Filipino accent, had
changed him, calmed him, and he suddenly felt warm and good and whole.

He wanted to write some more, but
felt too tired. He needed his rest. His
eyes were heavy and he had to strug-

gle to concentrate as he looked down at the photo and the Valentine on his lap. He smiled at the prospects of seeing them. He was almost there. A few hours more and Morang would be back with help. He looked over at the cave entrance and wondered how many hours had elapsed. With the coming of the morning light, the American medics would no doubt arrive.

Miguel and Rios were nearby watching him. They wouldn't let anything happen.

Neil looked again toward the entrance to the cave and saw the light. It must be morning. The rays of the sun seemed to radiate and call to him personally. Gently. It was the best he could remember feeling. He was going to make it now. His hand trembled as he held the crucifix up to the light and felt his senses sharpen. "The crown," he whispered, "the crown has thorns . . . even He—"

Neil's eyes opened wide, then slowly closed. They opened again, with the look of a very tired man who deserved a rest. He smiled and whispered, almost inaudibly, "Though I walk through the valley of the shadow . . ."

There was a gentle sigh. His face went still as a shallow rush of air escaped from his lungs.

Rios and Miguel looked on. Miguel bowed his head between his knees. Rios shook his head, walked over to Tomás, and picked up the picture, which now had slipped from Neil's hand and fallen beside him. He safely stored the letter in the ammo box. Rios took the Valentine card that held the C-ration creation—Tomás' good luck charm. He added the photo with it and reverently placed it back in the American's tattered shirt pocket. He secured the pocket, buttoning it, and patted Tomás' chest gently. "A good heart there," he whispered. He would give the box to the first American officer he met. Now he had a job to do.

He motioned to Miguel, who rushed forward to help, then noticed the Japanese officer's crucifix still clutched in the American's hand. Freeing it gently, he turned back and gave it to Miguel to put with Captain Ito's personal effects.

The two of them laid the body of the American flat on the floor of the cave, wrapping it tightly in the blanket. It had turned dark outside. In the morning he would bury him, next to the Jap who had cost him his life. Rios studied the still-warm face of the pilot. An undeniable peace masked the frigid triumph of death on the American.

He was a good man, Rios thought. "What a waste," he said out loud in Tagalog to Miguel. "Tomorrow the Americans come. But not until we bury him and I kill another Jap. For Tomás," the angry Filipino swore.

U.S.N. Special Delivery

Monday, February 2, 1998
Pasadena, California

It was 5:00 P.M. I had made dinner reservations for 6:00 at La Golondrina, and needed to pick Susan up at her hotel. Even though I'd spent the better part of Saturday afternoon and evening with her, just two days before, I couldn't wait to see her again. I looked at myself in the mirror, slipping a tie around my neck, and told myself it was time to admit I had fallen in love. I smiled at the thought; then Diane's face flashed through my mind.

Diane, I prayed silently, *if this is what
you want for me, if you want me to love
again, please—give me a sign.*

"Aren't you supposed to be leaving,
Dad?" my son, Eric, said.

Eric, now a freshman in college, and Rachel, a high school senior, were standing
in the bedroom doorway, grinning at me as
I fumbled to straighten my tie.

"Here. Let me help," Rachel said, walking toward me. She straightened the knot,
then patted it into place, and gave me a
kiss on the cheek.

"You look great, Dad," Eric said. "What
coat are you wearing?"

"The tweed wool," I said. "That's all right,
isn't it?" I added, suddenly unsure.

"Yeah, it'll look great. Quit worrying,
Dad," Eric said, pulling it out of my closet.
"You're gonna knock her eyes out," he
added, laughing.

"Thanks, Son, but this is business. I'm
just taking her to dinner before we meet
the crew at the train station. No big deal,"
I added, trying to sound believable.

"Yeah, right," Rachel said. "Come on,
Dad," she went on, "you've been talking
about Susan for two weeks. She sounds

perfect for you. She obviously likes you. So why don't you just admit that you like her and go for it? Mom would want you to."

"Oh, I don't know about that," I said, stealing a glance at her, wondering if she'd read my mind. Dismissing it as coincidence, I looked in the mirror one more time and turned to tell them good night.

"I don't know what I'd do without you guys. I hope you know that."

"Yeah, Dad. We do," Eric said, acting embarrassed. Rachel just smiled.

We went downstairs together. They both had studying to do and were settling down to their books as I went out the front door.

I arrived at the hotel right on time. Susan was waiting for me in the lobby. She looked striking, wearing white slacks and jacket over a jade blouse, the white a stunning contrast to her long black hair.

She greeted me with a happy smile, then took my arm as I led her out the door, saying she'd been looking forward to this all day. "Me too," I said, my heart leaping.

It was just getting dark as we arrived at the restaurant. It had rained earlier, and the winter air was clear. The stars would be out tonight. I pulled up to valet parking, then led her inside.

Vincente, the manager at La Golondrina, seemed to be waiting for us, standing just inside the door. He recognized me immediately. I hadn't been there for a while, but had gone there regularly for years with Diane and the kids—almost a family tradition. The food was excellent, the atmosphere comfortable yet romantic, and the music a mix of mariachi and contemporary soft rock.

"Señor Thomas, it has been a long time," he greeted warmly.

"Too long, Vincente. It's good to see you again," I said, shaking his hand.

"I have a special place reserved for you. I hope you like it, señorita."

"I'm sure I will," Susan replied, smiling at him as he motioned us into the dining room.

My heart began pounding as he led us across the room, seating us at a cozy table in the corner near the stage and the dance floor. It had been "our" table—mine and Diane's. Could this be a sign, I wondered? Of course not. Don't be silly. Vincente simply remembered our favorite table. I shook my head imperceptibly, trying to shake the emotions that had swept over me, then opened the menu.

"This is really nice, Neil," Susan began, pulling me back to the present. "I love authentic places. It gets boring eating *nouvelle cuisine* night after night on the road. Thank you for bringing me here." Her eyes seemed to sparkle.

The waiter took our order. After he'd left the table, Susan leaned toward me and crossed her arms on the table. "I've finished the story of your parents. It's beautiful . . . but I'm not sure what to think. How much of it is true, I mean, in detail?"

"You mean the ending, don't you?" I replied, remembering that I'd told her before that I'd taken liberties in relating the final scene.

"Of course!" she said, as if I were teasing. "It's a wonderful story, full of so much meaning, hope, and promise, but the ending is so incredible it's hard for me to fathom. I want to believe it. I want to believe it with all my heart. I'm really trying," she continued, her voice softening, "so don't laugh at me, but I'd like to hear it from your mouth."

"I would never laugh at you," I said, looking directly into her eyes, my expression as serious as I could make it. "Just tell me what you want to hear again."

"Tell me about the day the package arrived—after David Jackson turned it over to the military."

Smiling, I began.

February 12, 1994
Caroline Thomas home, Pasadena,
California

I had come to visit with Mom at the old home on Marengo, as was my custom. Really just to check on her, after school was out. It was on my way home to my condo on Cordova. She was starting to forget things and had been ill. First one thing, then another. She would battle her arthritis, then catch a cold; now she had just gotten over a serious bout with pneumonia. I worried how long she would be able to live alone, but she was still a tiger.

There was a knock on the door. I went to open it and saw two navy officers standing there with their backs to me. They quickly turned to greet me.

"Yes, gentlemen. What can I do for you?" I asked.

"Is this the home of Caroline Jensen Thomas?" the senior officer asked. He was a tall, slender man with dark hair— a strikingly modern version of what my father must have looked like in his navy duty uniform. He bore a distinctive smile that at once silently evoked the sentiment of friendship. I was taken aback for a moment.

"Yes. That's correct," I stuttered as a warm scented breeze seemed to wisp past me and into the small living room.

"May we come in?" the officer in charge politely asked, as they both took their hats off and moved toward the door at my invitation.

"Sir, is Mrs. Thomas in? We'd like to have a moment with her. Excuse me," he extended his hand in greeting, "my name is Brady, Richard Brady, Chaplain, United States Navy—and this is Chief Petty Officer Adashek."

The petty officer reached around

Chaplain Brady and offered a pleasant smile and firm handshake.

"Thomas, Neil Thomas, Jr. Pleased to meet you. Yes, please come in. My mother is home. She's resting. Please—" I gestured to the living room and they eased down on the sofa by the fireplace.

"Well, Mr. Thomas," the tall officer said, "this is going to be a doubly pleasant visit for us today."

I smiled, having no idea why they had come. "I'll go into her bedroom and check to see if she's awake. Just a moment, please."

Crazy thoughts about my father went through my head and my heart was pounding with increasing excitement. It had to be some very interesting news, but what? I tiptoed into the small hallway that led to my mother's bedroom and gently pushed the old raised panel door open to peek inside. She was sound asleep, stretched out on top of the covers fully dressed. As I gazed at one of the most beautiful women in my world, I wondered if someday soon I wouldn't find her there, just like she was now, in a sleep that no one could wake her from.

She was fatigued from the latest round of pneumonia and the growing chronic pain from the rheumatoid arthritis that caused her joints to swell and ache. I returned to the living room.

"I'm afraid you'll have to excuse me, gentlemen. We weren't expecting a visit. My mother is sound asleep. She's suffered from an illness and lately it's taken an especially large toll on her energy. How can I be of assistance to you?"

"Mr. Thomas, this visit is an especially pleasant task for me and Petty Officer Adashek. Occasionally we are called upon, by the navy, to visit families that have lost a loved one while in the service of their country. But this time we—"

Just then Chaplain Brady and Adashek stood, as if at attention, and smiled in the direction of the hallway. I turned around to see my mother walking slowly toward us with the aid of her cane.

"Mom, you okay?" I asked, rushing to

put my arm around her and guide her to a chair opposite the sofa, where the two men from the navy stood. I gestured to my mother to sit down. "Here, have a seat, Mom," I said.

She just stood there, still groggy, and seemed to be trying to focus on the tall man who stood smiling at her with outstretched hand. Her eyes strained to focus as she suddenly grabbed my arm for support. "Neil?" her soft high-pitched voice inquired in an unsteady tone.

"Yes, Mom. I'm right here," I replied. She continued to stare in fixed amazement at the two men dressed in white waiting to shake her hand.

"Mrs. Caroline Thomas?" Chaplain Brady asked formally.

My mother nodded. "I am Caroline Thomas."

"My name is Richard Brady, Commander, United States Navy. And this is CPO Daniel Adashek." The two men reached out and shook hands with her. "We are here with some very good news for you."

"Please? Won't you sit down?" she

asked sweetly, as I helped her to be seated. Her attention was focused as I had rarely seen it focused before. I was overcome with a sense of anticipation that a special, pivotal moment, one of those rarest of moments in life, was about to take shape and touch my mother, and me, for the rest of our lives.

As she fixed her eyes on the tall chaplain she seemed to glow with a radiance I had rarely seen in the last few pain-filled years of her life. A broad smile graced her lips and her face seemed to lighten, adding to the dimension of energy building in the room.

"Neil," she whispered softly.

"Yes, Mother?" I answered.

"Neil," she said again in a breath so low it was barely heard by anyone. I perceived it wasn't me, now, she was talking to.

"Ma'am, I am delighted to extend to you some news with regards to your husband, Lt. Neil Thomas, Sr."

A gasp rose from my mother's throat as her right hand went to her mouth and tears immediately welled up in her eyes.

The chaplain continued with a gentleness and a smile that seemed palpable. A sacred moment was about to take place. "On behalf of the United States Navy, I can extend to you the news that you have waited many years to hear. The body of your husband, Lt. Neil Thomas, Sr., listed as missing in action for almost fifty years, has been found." My mother and I hung on to every word that sprang from the chaplain's lips.

"What's more, I am delighted to deliver to you this package." He reached over to the petty officer, who handed him a thick, padded manila envelope marked "Special Duty Delivery, USN."

"I believe its contents will bring you much satisfaction and offer many answers about your husband's last months of life."

The silence was broken by a muffled cry as my mother, hands shaking, received the large envelope from the gentle chaplain. She fought the tears to no avail—and I found myself also searching for a way to keep that stolid composure befitting a man in control. It was no use. I, too, was overcome as my throat suddenly burned with effort to control the tears I failed to hold back. I moved next to my mother and gently laid a hand on her shoulder. The affectionate touch of a son for his mother was more defining than any words. We both knew he was coming home, and somehow we felt he knew it, too.

I looked up to my mother, who was staring far off into the distance as if she were gazing right through the walls of the small room. Her face revealed a serenity and joy that I didn't want to disturb—but I knew that there was more, and I wanted her to hear it. Silence reigned for a long moment as I gently coaxed my mother back into the awareness that we needed to listen to further information from the navy officers.

So I broke the magical silence. "What can you tell us? How was his body discovered?" I asked simply.

Commander Brady then went into details of retired Colonel Jackson's dis-

covery of the ammo box. Then the startling facts regarding my father's three
and a half months of survival in the
Philippine jungles as a companion to
Filipino guerrillas during the liberation
of the island nation during World War II.

"I'm delighted to inform you, Mrs.
Thomas, that the package you hold
contains letters from your husband,
and that they will further answer all of
the questions you may have regarding
his last days. He was a true hero, Mrs.
Thomas."

"Thank you. Thank you, boys—thank
you from the bottom of my heart." She
pulled the package away from her
chest and placed it with trembling
hands on her lap.

Chaplain Brady intervened. "Before
you open it, I should advise you of
something that will further be a comfort
and source of satisfaction to you. I
have been authorized to inform you
that the following awards have been
recommended by the secretary of the
navy on behalf of a grateful nation for
heroic actions performed by your hus-

band while in the service of his country. He handed me an envelope addressed to her from the Secretary of the Navy, Washington, D.C.

I opened it and began to read it aloud for her. It was dated two days before.

February 10, 1994

Dear Mrs. Thomas:

I am honored to inform you that your husband, Lt. Neil Thomas, Sr., killed in action during the campaign to liberate the Philippines from Japan during World War II, has been formally rec-ommended to receive your country's gratitude in the form of military honors and decorations.

For meritorious conduct in the face of the enemy and for gallantry above and beyond the call of duty, Lt. Neil Thomas, Sr., USN, will be posthu-mously awarded a Purple Heart, the Navy Cross, and the Congressional Medal of Honor.

In this, the forty-ninth anniversary year of the end to the Second World

War, it brings the Department of the Navy special satisfaction to inform you of these awards with the knowledge that your husband did not die in vain, but as a hero, truly distinguishing himself above the ordinary man.
Truly yours,

"*Signed, the Secretary of the Navy,*" I finished. I looked up into the beaming face of my mother as she let out a heavy sigh. "The Congressional Medal of Honor," I said, looking into my mother's eyes.

She nodded happily, like a child who had made a wonderful discovery. Her smile was different, like no other I'd ever seen before. This smile was connected with the sparkle in her eyes—a sparkle that only lovers know. It was a moment for her to savor, unlike any she had tasted for fifty years.

"He's coming home, Son! He's coming home like he said he would!" She was resolute in her statement and so innocent about its surety that all I could do was agree.

"I know he will. Sure he will, Mom." There was no sense in trying to dissuade her from her fantasy. It was a well-earned fantasy for a man lost for so many years.

"Mrs. Thomas," Commander Brady said, seeking her attention. "We have some additional information for you. We've received word from our forensics lab in Hawaii that all necessary work was completed Tuesday at 6:00 P.M. Pacific Standard Time. As soon as we knew for certain the remains found were in fact those of your husband, all arrangements for transporting his body home, and the other military data for processing benefits and military decorations, were put into motion. Based upon the latest information I received, his remains will arrive February 14th at Los Angeles International Airport. We're happy to inform you that, if you should request it, Lieutenant Thomas's remains may be interred, at no cost to you, in the Los Angeles Veterans' Cemetery in Westwood. If you have another choice for burial, you may let us know. I'll leave you my card.

"I want to assure you that this visit has been one of the highlights of my military career," he continued. "As a pilot myself, I know how deeply satisfying it is to pilots to know how hard their country strives to reunite lost men with their families. And because I know Lieutenant Thomas is alive in spirit, he must be smiling from ear to ear to know that he's finally coming home to rest. Congratulations, Mrs. Thomas, on this long deserved good news."

My mother nodded and thanked both men. I could see she was still trying to fathom what all this meant, and I was still stunned myself.

"I want to thank you," I said. "I can't tell you what this means to us. I'd like to thank Colonel Jackson as well. Can you tell me how I might contact him?"

"I have that information right here, sir," Petty Officer Adashek announced. He opened up his briefcase and handed me a slip of paper with the colonel's address and telephone number.

My mother sat still, staring at the package in her lap. A smile lingered on her face. I was sure that, in her mind, she was visiting another time and place.

We thanked the officers again, and my mother suddenly stood up, full of vigor and enthusiasm. She reached for Petty Officer Adashek's hands and cupped them in hers.

"I want you to know that you have made an old woman happier than she's been for fifty years." She looked into his eyes and whispered it again, "Thank you once again."

She moved to the chaplain then and took his hand, repeating the same phrase.

"No, my thanks to you, Mrs. Thomas," he said. "You're an inspiration and I'll never forget these moments we've shared."

A decorated veteran, wearing both wings and the cross on his uniform, Commander Brady looked as grateful as he claimed. He had been able to bring good news to someone for a change. He gave my mother a parting hug, then I escorted them to the door.

Chaplain Brady smiled as he looked up at the fifty-year-old hand-carved sign over the entry door. "Belief, the substance of things hoped for . . ." he read, then finishing, turned to me. "Now you have 'evidence of things not seen.' Congratulations again, Mr. Thomas."

He was right. I was stunned by the remarkable analogy to my father's life and the hope that my mother had always maintained—that she would hear from him again—that he would keep his promise to return to her.

Once they left I sat beside my mother on the sofa, and we opened the padded manila envelope. She sat there like a child on Christmas Day, and it occurred to me that this *was* a gift. I opened it with deep respect, reaching carefully to free the bundle inside.

The contents slid gently out onto the coffee table in front of us. On top of the neatly stacked envelopes was one with the message, "Open first." I complied.

Inside was a chain with old military dog tags. I pulled it out and held it out for my mother to see. She burst into quiet sobs and held the small metal tags to her lips. Dangling from the chain was another token of my father's identity—his crucifix.

All of a sudden, the passage of the years had been sealed. It was over. He had left, almost fifty years earlier to the day, and these tokens brought him back. It was a moment of triumph for my mother, who had patiently believed that he would return.

Each of his letters had been placed in a neat, new security envelope. I slowly opened the first one, and realized I'd be reading something that had been written five decades earlier. I gently pulled out a weathered and soiled onion-skin envelope and pulled back the flap to view its contents. It was a letter to my mother, dated February 13, 1945.

My Darling Caroline,

I'm sorry that on our wedding anniversary I cannot keep my promise to come home to you. But I pray this letter will find you safe and loving me still.

I wish I could tell you how much this awful business of war has changed me. Can a man draw closer to God

*through the hellish nightmare and con-
flict I've experienced? Can a man dis-
cover what really matters most through
the contrast of war and peace? I think
I have.*

*I now believe that knowing what mat-
ters most in life is the key to happiness.
You and Neil Junior are what matter
most to me.*

*But there's another key as well. I've
found that I can love and I can hate,
but never at the same time. I've also
found that I can only "be" one or the
other. Allowing myself to be filled to
any degree with hate destroys a por-
tion of the loving man I am, the man I
want to be.*

*I'm not sure I'm making any sense,
but I'm sure of what I want, of who I
am, and of what I hope to be—what I
hope for the world. For little Neil.*

*I had the words to a poem going
through my head. I thought they might
describe my concern and love for you,
but I have to tell you in my own words.
I had hoped to whisper that Bing
Crosby song, the one you liked so well,
into your ear today.*

I feel so alone in this dark cave. You are my light, sweetheart. If I could just see you, feel you . . . If you were here, this stench-filled cave would be transformed into a castle.

I have to go, but never doubt my deepest love for you.
Forever your loving husband,
   Neil

My eyes were brimming with tears. My mother took the letter from my hand, held it to her breast, saying, "I love you too, darling! I love you, too . . . I love you forever, darling."

The meaning of the event was evidenced by the miracle that had taken place. In two days, it would be their anniversary. Their fifty-first. The day my father's remains would be returning home.

As I considered the strange and sudden turn of events, my mother whispered something to me. I put my arm around her frail shoulders and asked, "What, Mom? What did you say?"

"I saw the swallow in the window

yesterday. It was there again today. I'm going with him when he comes home, Son. He's coming for me . . . I know he is. *La golondrina*."

Susan's eyes were filled with tears as I finished, my voice filled with emotion. She said she still wanted to hear me tell her the ending again, what happened at Union Station, but it didn't matter anymore if every detail was true. She said she was beginning to understand the deeper meaning in the story, that what mattered most was its message. Of course, she was right.

I felt as though we'd been sitting there for hours, but a glance at my watch told me we still had plenty of time to eat, then walk across the street to Union Station long before the crew arrived. I wanted to be alone with her there for a while. I'd be happy to relate the story of what finally happened that day, February 14, 1994, and I could see with my own eyes just how much she wanted to believe.

We ate in comfortable silence to the music of the mariachis, watching people dance as we enjoyed our food. Susan

seemed to be enjoying herself, more relaxed than she'd been since I met her.

Just as we finished our meal, the band
stopped playing. The mood in the restaurant shifted considerably as the dancers
left the floor and an old Classics IV song
from the sixties began playing over the
speakers.

Faded photographs, covered now
with lines and creases.
Tickets torn in half, memories in bits
and pieces.
Traces of love, long ago . . . that didn't
work out right,
Traces of love, with me tonight.

My heart raced at the song, the same
one that had played here the night I asked
Diane to marry me, then my face turned
white when Susan chose Diane's exact
words to ask me to dance.

"Any chance of me talking you into a
dance?"

As I stood, taking her hand to lead her
out to the dance floor, I said a silent "thank
you" to my wife . . . Diane.

The Last Valentine

Monday evening, February 2, 1998
Union Station, Los Angeles, California

We left La Golondrina with an hour to spare before Susan's CNTV crew would arrive. My head was still spinning, and I felt as if I were walking on air, now certain that my feelings for her were right. She wasn't the same person I'd met just a few weeks before, and I desperately wanted to believe that she felt the same way about me, but I couldn't be sure. The interview was tomorrow, and I only had one day left to find out.

We crossed Alameda, and I opened the door to the old Union Station. The moment we stepped inside, I knew she could feel its magic. She stopped, just inside the door, turning to me with a look of childlike wonder in her eyes.

"Neil . . . it's even more wonderful than I imagined," she said, her voice hushed, her eyes taking everything in at once. "It really does seem to be frozen in time, like you said in the story."

"Yeah, I know. Come on, let me show you around."

The old station was nearly deserted. Our footsteps echoed as we walked. I showed Susan the old ticket booth, then the photo gallery, where she lingered for a long moment over the one that had captured my parents' good-bye.

"Show me the chair where your mother waited each year," she finally said, turning around.

"We're headed there now."

"It's exactly as you described." We had reached the old leather-backed chair. She was caressing its arm, facing the tunnel. When she sat down, with a look of anticipation on her face, she softly announced,

"I want to feel what Caroline felt. Neil, tell me the ending. Here. Now."

I sat next to her and we both stared into the distant tunnel as I unfolded the final Valentine story to her.

February 14, 1994
Union Station, Los Angeles, California

Josiah had returned from checking on a disturbance in the parking lot fronting on Alameda Street.

Armando, the custodian, stopped him. "Say, Josiah, I just passed the old lady. You know, Caroline? She doesn't look so good. You better go check her out."

"Thanks, Mando." He gave his Union Station friend a playful punch and hurried up the wide aisle to Caroline's seat.

"How we doin', Miss Caroline?" he asked. She had drifted off to sleep. He wanted to make sure that was all it was.

"Oh, Josiah. I was having the most delightful dream," she replied in her characteristic high-pitched voice, which wavered ever so slightly as she opened her eyes from her catnap.

"Sorry to disturb you, Miss Caroline, but just checkin' on you like I promised."

"Josiah, you're never a bother. Can you tell me what time it is?"

He had bent his knees so he could be at eye level with her as they talked. "It's 2:35 P.M., Miss Caroline. How long you plannin' to stay before goin' back home?" he asked, in a concerned tone.

"Neil should be here by 3:00 P.M. to get me. That's when the navy said he was returning to Los Angeles."

Josiah looked puzzled. Neil Jr. must have taken a train out of town, and knowing that his mother came here every year, he must be returning on Amtrak from somewhere. Oh, well. He'd take care of her until Neil showed up. Caroline was getting old, and no doubt living heavily in the past. After all, that's why she came to Union Station every year on Valentine's Day.

"Well, honey, I be checkin' as usual. If Neil don't come for you, I'll be glad to give you a ride home. You can count on it." He got up, tipped his hat and smiled as he patted her shoulder. He noticed an old weathered envelope in her lap. Must be an old letter her husband sent from the war, he thought.

"No need, but thank you anyway, Josiah. Please let my son, Neil, know I love him when you see him." She did look a little pale and did act unusually tired, but at the same time she seemed to radiate a serenity and a happiness he had never seen before.

Josiah scratched his head and shook it sadly. "Sure thing, little lady. Sure thing." He hated to see her lose her mental stamina, her memory and touch with reality. Her obvious exhaustion and poorer health than the previous year worried him.

"I'll be right back, Miss Caroline. You rest, I got a call to make."

Whether or not the woman's son was coming to get her, he thought, he was going to call the Union Station nurse to have her check on Mrs. Thomas.

She looked down at the last letter that Neil had written, scratched quickly on a piece of carton-type paper on

February 14, 1945. She had read and then reread all of his letters, and now understood clearly why he couldn't come home fifty years ago. She understod him better, too. She understood that the war had changed him and that, like the letter from the secretary of the navy had said, he was not an "ordinary man." He had learned the secrets of love and had possessed the strength of character to employ the principles even when it wasn't convenient. He gave his life for someone else. She was proud, so very proud. His letters from the ammo box were a monument to their love and, if the last Valentine she had given him when they tearfully parted many years ago was missing, she knew there had to be a good reason.

She hadn't eaten, she couldn't sleep, and now all that was catching up with her. Yesterday she had seen the swallow in the window and knew she could go with him when he returned. Then last night the dream came back. He came back in it.

It had happened as she slept with his

last letter, the crucifixes and dog tags held tightly to her breast. In the dream she was working in their garden. She was young, and she somehow knew that he was coming home from his last mission. She remembered how he had disappeared into the fog bank with the question on his mind, "Can you do it, Caroline?" That was a dream fifty years old, a recurring dream that had sustained her for all those years. But now . . . now she was an old woman, and she had done all she could; and in this new dream she appeared young again, like no time had passed at all.

In the dream, she thought about his question, Can you do it, Caroline? and she had strongly replied, Yes! I can! I did! She had survived the heartache, the disappointments, and she had been strong—for him. Now he had to come back. She had done her part; their son was reared. She was ready to go with him.

She remembered that she had looked over her shoulder in the dream. She was in the garden tending to the roses, the same ones they had planted together five decades earlier. A light filled the mist, the fog behind her. She saw him. He slowly walked out of the fog with a bright bouquet of the most beautiful flowers she had ever seen. He was as handsome as he ever had been and she let go of the roses and pierced her hand on one of the thorns. Then he ran to her and pulled her to him tenderly, kissed her hands, and the bleeding stopped. They embraced and kissed again. His smile consumed her. Then she woke up.

Now she waited. She sat in those same seats where they had earlier waited for his boarding call to go to war. They faced gates G and H, the two gates that opened to the tunnel. She was glad it was there where she would see him. Nothing, not even death itself, could hold her back from him.

February 14, 1994—2:30 P.M.
Caroline Thomas home, Pasadena,
California

I opened the door of my mother's house to find it was empty. I suspected the worst. She was in no condition to make the trip to Union Station by bus. She had worn herself out over the preceding two days—had hardly slept, hadn't eaten. Her heart was weak. She had suffered three minor heart attacks with the pneumonia over the past year.

I had made it clear to her that I would get out of school early and pick her up and take her to LAX to meet the plane.

The navy chaplain, Commander Brady, had called the night before to confirm the time. The plane would arrive at 3:00 P.M. We would be met there by him and reporters. He suggested that we should not arrive too early. He wanted to make sure the reporters didn't cause any confusion for my mother. The chaplain also said he would be sure to allow my mother and me the space we needed to celebrate the moment, a most sacred moment. A husband, father, and war hero was returning home; and we deserved the privacy to savor it, the chaplain had said.

I had made sure to call her in the morning to remind her, and had even left a note on the refrigerator. I could

hardly believe she would misunder-
stand. I had gone so far as to say that
on our return trip from LAX we would
swing by Union Station so she could
spend some moments there and keep
her traditional rendezvous with the
past.

As I headed back out the door to
leave, I saw the note taped to the back
of it. I quickly read it:

Dear Son,
I want you to know that I went ahead
to look for your father. Everything is in
order. I'm happier than I've been in fifty
years. I love you so much. You have
been my life, and without you I couldn't
have gone on. Look out the bedroom
window. See how the royal red rose
blooms early? Just like it did fifty years
ago. The swallow returned today. I'll be
okay. I'll always love you. Forever. Be
faithful and love the Lord. Forever is a
promise to keep. Your father said that.

Happy Valentine's Day
Mom

I put the note gently down on the small table next to the mail drop. I wanted to know for myself that it was true. I walked back into her bedroom to see. Looking out the window, I saw a single red rosebud had opened.

I would have to hurry. I knew where to find her. My mother was a sweet woman, but a stubborn one when she wanted to be. I suspected that this wasn't stubbornness, however. It was confusion. Clearly the last few years showed she was becoming more confused and forgetful, and the last few days had taken a toll on her. I would have to drive fast and hope that there were no traffic problems on the 110 Pasadena Freeway.

As I closed the door behind me, I felt as though it would never open again to find my mother there. I knew she had found a love at the end of her life equally as exquisite as the love at the beginning. And somehow I sensed that what I would find at Union Station was at the same time my greatest fear and her greatest hope. Could an old woman who loved her life away finally find peace?

February 14, 1994—2:55 P.M.
Union Station, Los Angeles, California

As Caroline rested there, immersed in dreams of how it had been, she recalled the days of loneliness. The melodies of music suddenly attracted her attention—strains of music coming from all around her. It was a familiar tune. One of her favorites, one of his—Neil used to sing it to her. Either her mind was playing tricks on her or the sounds of the old Bing Crosby tune really did fill her ears.

Because you speak to me—I find the roses round my feet, and I am left with tears and joy of thee!
Because God made thee mine—I'll cherish thee, through all life and darkness, and all time to be.
And pray his love may make our love divine—Because God made thee mine!

She smiled as she looked down at the letter in her lap. Her dress seemed to be the red flower-patterned dress, the one she had worn the day they said good-bye. Her leg, the arthritic, crippled one, was young and strong-looking. The shoes with the square toes were the same ones she'd worn that day. With eyes closed, she reached her hand up to her face. Her skin was firm and smooth. Then she opened her eyes to look again—to see if it was all just a dream. She turned to see a bright light filling the tunnel.

The outlined form of someone walking from the tunnel—walking toward the gate, toward her—seemed radiant, causing her to focus sharply with an ability her normal sight had never experienced.

She was surprised at the light filling the waiting area. It was unlike any she had seen, and it was coming from both outside and inside the large room. She looked above her and it was there. She looked beneath her and the light was there, too.

Caroline felt drawn somehow toward

the tunnel, toward the gates leading to the tunnel and the tracks. She had never felt such an euphoric sense of wellness—wholeness. Her eyes saw things differently. If it were a dream, she would refuse to wake up.

She wasn't sure what to think. She didn't care. There wasn't a word to describe the childlike sense of adventure that possessed her. Then her eyes seemed to open wider. She saw more than she had ever been able to with her aging eyes. Someone familiar . . .

He's looking for me! "Neil! Here! At the end of the tunnel!" she involuntarily called out. "I'm here, Neil, I'm here!" she shouted, as she flew from her seat to go to him. She felt light, ethereal, alive. There was no heaviness to her legs holding her down now. Her husband, Lt. Neil Thomas, Sr., stood there, smiling, in his dress white navy uniform. He was holding a beautiful bouquet of roses in one hand, a card in the other.

He was there. He had come for her. It was just like it was then. The palpable love between them, fifty years before—but the intensity was elevated—melodious!

His arms were outstretched. His smile, the same as she remembered.

"Oh, Neil! Darling, I love you. I love you!" she cried. She threw herself into his arms and let all her emotions out as he held her tightly. She wept. Could it be a dream?

"No, sweetheart, it's not a dream." Neil whispered the words in her ear. He let her release all her feelings as he held her, smiling down at his woman. He stroked her long auburn-colored hair that cascaded once more around her shoulders.

He whispered to her. "I'll never let you go again, Caroline. Never, darling." He kissed her tenderly as they embraced. "I'm sorry I'm late, but I've always been there—with you and our son. Watching, day after day, caring." He held her by the waist and caressed her cheeks with his, sweeping the tears from her soft face.

"You did it, Caroline! You handled the thorns. You brought me back to you." He softly spoke to her in tones that soothed, deep resonating tones that filled her with assurance and peace. He pointed back to the waiting area and the chair. She didn't want to let her eyes leave his face—just in case it was, indeed, all nothing more than a dream.

"Look, Caroline. Look at the chair. Look!" At his gentle insistence she took her eyes off him and looked, just for a split second.

Sitting there was a vaguely familiar appearance, the old woman she had become. That was her cane, her purse, and . . .

Her eyes went back to his face—and she smiled, reaching around his neck to kiss him over and over. The years melted away as if the lovers had never been separated.

"You came for me. I knew you would come, darling." She beamed as they looked into each other's eyes and communicated with a language unheard—unspoken.

He handed her the bouquet and said, "Look down toward the end of the tunnel." She looked—and there was light, more light than she had ever seen. It filled her with a sense of ecstasy beyond anything she could have ever dreamed. It was pure, it was real, and it beckoned.

"Caroline, we have to go now." He gripped her hand and gestured for her to come with him. The words had a familiar ring to them. The last time he had said those words, she had passed through the tunnel with him—and he had not returned. This time, though . . .

"Wait until you see where I got these roses! Wait until you see the other side of the tunnel."

Not track twelve? she thought, as she looked up into his face.

"No, not track twelve," he grinned. "Remember when we stood here fifty years ago with hundreds of servicemen and their wives and girlfriends?"

"Yes," she replied with a broad smile.

"You didn't want to go into the tunnel, and I whispered something into your ear?"

She laughed. It had all come back to her. His sense of humor, his wit. He was the same Neil, only—

"Remember?" He held her close to him as he had then. She put her face against his chest.

"Yes," she returned softly. "I remember. I remember it all, and it doesn't hurt anymore. You said, the tunnel of love." She looked up at him as their hands joined.

"Sweetheart—more love than you have ever known. More love than I can explain. And it goes on forever. I've always loved you, Caroline. Now I always will."

Her mind sped swiftly back in time, to the words he'd whispered to her then as he said them to her again, in this same place—the noise of the train engines filled the station and he shouted it. Now the words were soft and serene as he repeated them.

"I've loved you since Adams School, through the years growing up in Eagle Rock, through all the good times, and now I can't remember any bad. I think I've just always loved you!"

He scooped her up into his arms as they melted into a long-awaited kiss and embrace. He gazed into the eyes of his young wife, then whispered into her ear as his cheek made contact with her tender skin. "Now I know what the feeling is when I used to say those words to you—when I used to try to describe how I felt—when I used to say, *Love isn't good enough. Not for you, Caroline.*"

Indescribable light and love . . . it filled her . . . She now, at the end of her life, knew a more powerful love than she'd known in the beginning. She turned to look back one last time at Union Station and the waiting area, a scene fading into the distance. There was Josiah, gently trying to shake her old body awake. There on her lap was Neil's last letter, the one that had arrived just two days before. And there also was . . . She beamed seeing it there!

The swallows seemed to sing to her from La Golondrina across the way, and sweet rhythms of music filled the air. She moved with her handsome young pilot as she watched the fading picture. She could barely still see the old lady resting in the chair . . . her chair . . . a faint smile gracing her face, and she knew everything would be okay.

The light was getting brighter now and they seemed to be walking into it. The warmth and glow now before them caused the dreariness of the old train station tunnel to completely disappear behind her.

"The roses, Neil. The place where you got them from. The stems, do they have . . . ?"

Smiling, he gestured toward a man and woman entering the tunnel. The man was dressed in some sort of military uniform with a high stiff collar and the woman was clothed in the most beautifully flower-patterned kimono-style dress.

The happy couple paused a few feet in front of them. Neil gestured toward them with his hand and the words Ito, a name, and *tomodachi,* a Japanese word, came so loudly that she instantly knew its translation.

Itos—our friends! she thought, which brought a smile of recognition to the faces of the two Japanese greeters.

The man smiled broadly and bowed reverently. The small woman came forward and handed Caroline another bouquet. The colors were beyond what she had ever seen in life!

Caroline examined the stems, then looked up to her husband and threw her arms around him. Finally, pulling back, she glanced at the bouquets in her hands and examined his face in a questioning gaze.

He smiled, stopping her, and then kissed her in a way she had never remembered. "No thorns. Never again. No . . . not on these. Come on, sweetheart. There's nothing more for you to do. It's time to go."

February 14, 1994—3:05 P.M.
Union Station, Los Angeles, California

My heart raced as I drove to the station, filled with a sense of dread. Something terrible had happened. Nothing else could explain why my mother hadn't come home in time for our trip to the airport. She wouldn't miss the most important day of her life—the day she'd been waiting fifty years for.

What happened next was surreal.

The moment I entered the station I knew I was experiencing something unique. The first thing I noticed was a light that seemed to be emanating from the far side of the station, near the main gate that led to the tracks. It wasn't a natural light. It was a light like no light I'd ever seen. I could not only see it, I could feel it. Warm, yellow, mild . . . indescribable.

Then I noticed Josiah. The old man was standing rigid, looking in the direction of this same light, which was now rapidly fading.

Though I found it hard to tear my attention away from the light, I realized he was standing at my mother's bench, the same bench she had occupied nearly all day every Valentine's Day for the past fifty years.

Then I saw her. Slumped to one side, not sitting in her usual upright way. I hurried to the bench. By now the light had completely disappeared, and

Josiah snapped out of his state of suspended animation.

"Mom!"

Her eyes were closed. Her face was graced with the most peaceful smile.

"I'm sorry, Mr. Thomas," Josiah was saying. "Your mother just . . ." The old man was so agitated, I put my hand on his arm to steady him.

"How long has it been? Josiah, answer me."

His eyes were filled with tears. "I don't know," he said. "A few minutes. I called the nurse. She got here, but there was nothing she could do. She went to call the Paramedics." He nodded toward the phone booth.

I knew the Paramedics were unnecessary, and told Josiah to call them off. He moved toward the phone booth, as I leaned toward my mother.

Her last letter from my father was still clutched in her hand, but that wasn't what had caught my attention. Something new, yet old . . . she held something else . . . something the navy, Chaplain Brady, hadn't delivered . . . I was sure, then, that he indeed had kept his promise to her.

I stopped, stood up, and looked down at Susan. I decided to test her feelings, to not reveal the evidence of love found with my mother's body. Not yet anyway.

"Belief is the substance of things hoped for, the evidence of things not seen." Susan stood, whispered the words, reaching for my hands. "Neil, I don't know what to say." The tears in her emerald eyes made them glisten with a light that reminded me of that light I'd seen in the station when I found my mother on her last Valentine's Day. It pulled me in.

"Don't say anything." I welcomed her toward me. I don't remember how our first kiss began, or when it ended. But I can still feel it. It was like slow dancing with eternity.

Epilogue

Tuesday, February 3, 1998
Pasadena, California

I pulled up in front of my mother's old house early Tuesday morning. A hint of rain was in the air, and the sky was clear. It promised to be another beautiful, Southern California winter day.

As I got out of the car, I noticed the real estate agent had been here sometime since Saturday evening. There was now a sign in the yard. Seeing it, a feeling of melancholy washed over me.

I had grieved over the loss of my

mother, yet rejoiced for her at the same time. For fifty long years, she'd held fast to her faith in the power of love, in the strength of a promise, waiting to see it fulfilled.

It had been three weeks since I'd first learned that my parents' story would be told on CNTV's *American Diary.* I had never dreamed that the world would hear it this way. I first started writing the story, one month after my mother's death, as a gift to my children. I wanted them to know what had happened, to learn through my parents' story that miracles do occur in this angry world of ours. To know that beyond our daily existence is something larger that defies understanding. If I could only show them that, while they were young, perhaps it would save them some pain.

Now, thanks to Craig Warren of CNTV and Susan Allison, the story of a love that transcended time and death would reach millions of people, and I felt humbled somehow.

I wandered into my mother's garden, caught up in my thoughts. I was anxiously anticipating the interview, hoping it would touch many lives, but I knew it might also be the end of my time with Susan. And the sign in the yard marked the end of a chapter in my life.

Now, as I walked through the garden, I realized something that had slipped past me before. On Friday, just four days earlier, I had come out to this garden and cut a bouquet of roses for Susan, and had overlooked that they had bloomed early this year. My father's prize roses, the ones he'd planted with so much care, the ones that hadn't bloomed early since the day of my mother's death, four years ago. My spirits lifted, knowing there was something special in this sign from nature, and my thoughts turned to Susan Allison.

I knew I wanted her in my life. After everything that had happened last night, I believed that she felt the same way, that we had been brought together for a reason. But we lived in different worlds. My roots were here; my memories were here. And my children were finally happy again. They were young, and their lives were just beginning. I couldn't ask them to give up their dreams for mine. Maybe Susan and I had met only to tell this story. And, if that were true, that would have to be enough.

I would be grateful for having had her in my life, if only for this purpose, this short time.

The sound of a car pulling into the drive snapped me back to the present. She had told me last night she wanted to come early today, before the crew arrived, saying she wanted to make sure everything was ready. When she said it, I'd hoped it was just an excuse to see me again, a chance for us to be alone one more time. Now, in the light of morning, I didn't feel so confident.

She was out of the car, walking toward me with a smile on her face, as I came around the side of the house.

"Good morning, Neil."

"Good morning, yourself," I said, returning her smile. "Wow! You look great," I went on, amazed that she seemed to keep getting more beautiful. She was dressed for the interview, wearing a crisp, green linen dress. Modest diamond earrings sparkled against the background of her dark hair.

"Thank you," she said, then quickly changed the subject as if I'd made her self-conscious. "So . . . are you ready for this?"

"Yeah. A little nervous, I guess, but I'm sure I'll be fine." I started toward the front of the house, thinking she'd be anxious to get inside, but she stopped me with a hand on my arm.

"We've got time for a walk in the rose garden. I'd like to see it again. Would you mind?"

"Not at all. I've been there all morning." I laughed. We turned toward the garden. "The roses, this variety, have a magic to them. They are early this year."

Susan was quiet at first, as if lost in her thoughts. We were in the middle of the garden before she spoke again. "I noticed the sign in the yard when I pulled up in the driveway. I know you've been packing and all, but I guess I didn't think you'd actually sell it. Guess I've been hoping you'd change your mind." She looked at the roses, then down at the ground.

I waited, holding my breath, wondering what else she was going to say.

"It's just that you've got so many wonderful memories here," she went on, "and the idea of strangers moving in is—well, it's awful." She'd been watching the ground, but looked up at me now. "I don't know how you can leave it behind."

My heart ached as she said it. I knew she was right. And in that moment, I realized what was missing in my life.

I was about to tell my parents' story to the world, and I wanted the world to believe it. I had witnessed a miracle, had proof that it happened, yet I hadn't believed miracles were possible for myself. I thought I was through with them, though, in truth, where love makes its presence known, there is never an end to miracles.

I remembered something Susan had said that first day we met. She'd said she could almost feel the love my mother had put in this house. Those ghosts I'd been running from weren't just bittersweet memories, but the spirit of love that lives on beyond the limitations of human existence, the love that transcends space and time. I had been running when I should have been embracing.

It was time to act upon my beliefs.

I snipped off a cardinal-colored rose at the stem and turned to face Susan, placing it in her soft, slender hand, which I'd taken in mine. She smiled down at the perfect flower, then looked up at me, a question in her eyes.

"What?" she said. "Tell me."

I found myself speechless. In a matter of seconds, I had emerged from the past and was ready to face an uncertain future. But I wasn't sure how to begin.

"Wait here for me, Susan. There's something I want you to see."

I released her hand, headed for the house. When I'd asked her to wait for me there, she agreed, looking baffled.

I walked to the living room and went to the mantel. I had placed the old photo from my parents' wedding there for the interview, along with a few other items I knew were important. I looked at the photograph now. They were smiling in happiness, as if urging me on. I thanked them silently for their help, picked up the old tattered envelope, then went back to where Susan was waiting, under the trellis among the early roses.

"Susan," I said as I reached for her hand again, "Do you believe in my story, that love never dies?"

"Don't you know the answer to that by

now?" she began. "If I didn't believe it was possible, I would never have kissed you last night. And it shouldn't make any difference if I believe it all happened—I know it's the meaning, it's the feeling beneath it all, that matters." She paused for a moment, her green eyes searching mine. "You've changed me, and I'll always be grateful for that."

"What about the last Valentine?" I asked.

"What do you mean?" she quizzed hesitatingly, but only for an instant. "Neil, I'm not asking for evidence. What I've felt, what I feel, from hearing your story, from knowing you—that's all I need."

"I said I had something to show you, remember?" Still holding her hand, I turned her palm up and gave her the frayed and faded envelope.

A puzzled expression crossed her face. "Go ahead," I said quietly. "See what's inside."

Her fingers were trembling as she opened the envelope. When she pulled out the antique Valentine, its back reinforced with a piece of old C-ration box, tears flooded her eyes and her porcelain skin seemed to turn even fairer.

"It can't be!" she whispered, her eyes filling with tears, her lips parting in a smile. Susan examined my parents' Valentine. Opening the card, she saw the cardboard trellis, fashioned from memory exactly like the trellis we were standing under now. There was the photograph my father dropped on the floor of the cave, moments before he died. My mother had replaced it with the photo he had sent her—of Lieutenant Thomas, holding this same Valentine, on board the USS *Princeton*.

"Yes, it can, Susan. It happened," I said. "He kept his promise to bring it back to her!"

She was holding the card, caressing the last of the crushed and fragile five-decades-old rose petals with her fingers. I lifted her chin with my hand. "Stay in this house with me, Susan. I want it to be filled with love again. I know you and I can fill it together."

"I love you, Neil Thomas. . . ."

I smiled as I witnessed tenderness filling her eyes with tears. My free arm went around her waist. She released her hand, the one that with mine had held the symbol of love, and put her arms around my neck. We embraced and, as our lips met again, our loneliness melted into joy. We were finally home—to love—with "Forever, a promise to keep."

Afterword

The Last Valentine is all about love, relationships, and the realization of what matters most in life. Because a great deal of the story is played out through the eyes of fictional characters who lived and loved during the era of World War II, much of the vocabulary and word usage from that time period are used in the dialogue.

A shortening of the proper "Japanese" to the epithet "Jap" is used strictly in the context of the times. The author is extremely sensitive to contemporary mores discouraging use of demeaning cultural and racial slang. However, in the context of the war years, and as represented in American media and jargon, the term "Jap" and other epithets accurately convey the tension and setting in which the story takes place.

The final outcome—the message—of *The Last Valentine* absolutely conveys my deepest sentiments and respect to those of Japanese ancestry.

This book is a work of fiction. Historical cities, places, and wartime events are used as a backdrop to the drama the characters are engaged in. In doing so, I have sought to impart a sense of reality with the hope that readers will find themselves transported in time to the events of the story and immersed in its emotions.

Though what I have written has been pieced together from encounters with real people, real places, and my own dreams, any similarity to actual events or people is entirely coincidental.